THE CAT CAPER

PET WHISPERER P I
BOOK 5

MOLLY FITZ

Cozy Mystery Cafe
www.CozyMysteryCafe.com

ABOUT THIS BOOK

What's even worse than having a snarky talking tabby as your best friend?

When he inexplicably goes missing...

Octo-Cat is gone, and all the evidence suggests that he was taken on purpose. With the growing number of people the two of us have put behind bars, it's no surprise that someone's out for revenge.

But how will I ever manage to solve this particular crime without the help of my partner?

The only other person who might be able to help me just relocated to Georgia. But I'm desperate enough to try anything, including exposing my secret to the whole of Blueberry Bay. Anything to bring him home safe.

Oh, Octo-Cat. Where have you gone?

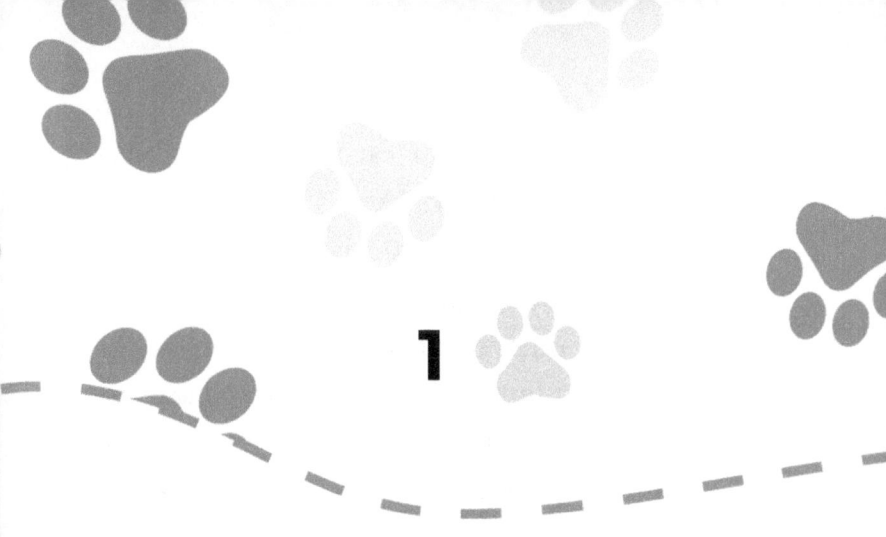

1

My name's Angie Russo, and I'm a cat person.

Lately, that is the most important thing about me.

Not that I'm a part-time paralegal and also a part-time private investigator. Not that I live in a giant East Coast manor house or that my quirky nan is one of my best friends. Not even the fact that I've managed to rack up seven associate degrees due to my academic indecisiveness.

Nope.

The most important thing about me is definitely the fact that I have a cat.

But he's not just any ordinary feline, mind you.

He talks. *A lot.* As in hardly ever shuts up.

And if you think your cat is demanding, just imagine what my life looks like.

I have to feed him a particular brand of food in a particular flavor in a particular Lenox dish and at very particular times of the day. He also only drinks Evian. I've tried to trick him in the past to save on this ridiculous expense, but—I kid you not—he knew the difference. And, boy, did I pay for that one.

In all honesty, I can spare the expense, though. You see, my cat also has a trust fund—a big one. His previous owner was murdered, and it was by pure dumb luck that he and I ended up together. That is, if you can call almost dying at the hands of a faulty coffee maker "luck."

I mean, I do.

I love my life and would change very little about it. I do plan to quit my paralegal gig soon to pursue detective work full-time. Naturally, my cat would be my partner in that operation. He watches so much *Law & Order* that he practically has an honorary degree in criminal justice, and he's got claws that he isn't afraid to use when we find ourselves in a tricky scrape.

Other than his sometimes gratuitous violence and over-the-top television addiction, he has plenty of other unique skills that make him an indispensable partner, too. First, there's the fact we can communicate. Obviously, no one ever suspects that the curious-looking feline across the way is actually listening in on their conversations.

When you add Nan to the mix with her background in Broadway and knack for creating colorful characters and then flawlessly bringing them to life, we have quite the little operation.

So, go ahead and eat your heart out, Scooby Doo.

If you're wondering about me and who I am outside of being a cat owner, I'll make this real simple for you: I'm the Velma of the group. I love researching, learning, wrapping my mind around any and every puzzle that comes our way.

I have a near-photographic memory and a knack for mnemonic devices, but lately my brain has been a tad less reliable than I'd like.

Usually, I remember everything without fail. Ever since this new guy Peter Peters started working at the law office, though, things have definitely gotten a bit fuzzy. I hated that guy almost instantly, and I'm pretty sure he has something to do with the fog that's taken up residence in my head... But I just can't remember why.

Lucky for me, he'll be leaving the state very soon. Unluckily, he's taking his cousin Bethany, a former partner at the same firm, with him. She was a good friend, and I'll definitely miss having her around. Still, I get the fact that she needs to be there for her family—even if this particular member of her family is the creepiest guy I have ever met.

Honestly, it's probably time for me to quit, anyway. Well, just as soon as I work up the nerve to let down my secret crush by handing in my two weeks' notice. I've had the hots for our senior partner, Charles Longfellow, III, ever since he moved here from California and began working his way up the ranks at our firm. He's only a few years older than me, a legal prodigy and also someone who's had a few lucky strokes like I have—so no judgment, please.

I'd probably have bitten the bullet and asked him out already, but he has a girlfriend now. By the way, I hate her, and not just because she's standing in the way of what I'm convinced could actually be true love, but because she's mean and bitter and has never shown me an ounce of kindness in our entire acquaintanceship.

At least she's not a murderer, although I did suspect her of a double homicide a few months back. We solved that one, though, and got both her and her brother off the hook. We also solved the murder of a prominent senator who used to live right next door.

And as ready as I am to hang up my sign as a full time P.I., I'd much rather be chasing white-collar criminals around town than the homicidal maniacs I've been dealing with as of late. Because that's the thing about murderers: they're dangerous with a capital *D*. It stands to reason that eventually one of them is going to want revenge on the crazy girl and her cat that got them arrested in the first place.

I just hope I'm ready when karma comes calling...

* * *

I almost ran straight into Nan when I returned home from work that sunny afternoon.

"Look what I made for you today in my community art class!" she cried, completely unbothered by the fact I'd almost knocked her into the antique stained-glass windows that flanked either side of our front door.

I took one giant step back and studied the

sizable metal sign she held between her aged hands.

"Pet Whisperer, P.I.," I read aloud, then grabbed the thing to take a closer look—and almost dropped it as soon as the heft transferred to my hands. "Oof, this is really heavy!"

Nan shook her head and tutted at me. "Well, it's not made of paper, dear."

"What kind of art class are you taking, anyway?" I said as I appreciated how the various scrap metals had come together to create something new and beautiful.

"It's a little bit of everything—sculpture, welding, landscapes, still-lifes, nudes." She winked at that last one, and I had no doubt that this meant the nudes were her entire reason for signing up in the first place.

"Sounds like a good time," I said with a laugh. My nan was always finding something new and exciting to occupy her time. Apparently, this included advertising my closely kept secret to all of Blueberry Bay.

Nan caught me studying the sign with a nervous expression and explained, "It's for your business, dear. Seeing as I'm your assistant, I figured I'd make myself useful."

"But we haven't even officially opened yet," I argued. I loved Nan and was excited she wanted to help, but the added pressure didn't make this big career transition any easier on me.

"Yes, you really do need to get on with it already," my grandmother told me as she furrowed her brow in my direction.

I groaned even though she was one-hundred percent right about this. "Okay, but I don't want people to know I talk to animals, remember?" That was the other weird thing about the last couple weeks.

My memory was a bit fuzzy, but also my mind seemed to be more open. I still didn't know how I could talk to Octo-Cat, but lately I'd been able to hear other animals besides him, too.

First there were the birds on the rooftop, then a curious squirrel in my garden. I'd even managed to listen in on a great big buck I'd startled in the woods outside our manor house. My ability to understand other animals was touch and go, and also a brand new complication in my already crazy life.

It had always been Octo-Cat and only Octo-Cat, and I really didn't know how I felt about becoming a full-on Dr. Dolittle these days. If word spread among the animal kingdom that I could understand their needs, would they all start swarming me with their legal problems?

I was way out of my depth here, considering I was just a paralegal and had no great passion for the law—other than choosing to uphold it most of the time in my day-to-day life.

"Where's Octo-Cat?" I asked, craning my neck to glance up the grand staircase but not finding him at the top. Normally, he liked hanging out up there this time of day because it was when the skylights dumped lots of warm sunlight in that exact spot.

"He's around here somewhere, I'm sure," Nan answered dismissively as she took the sign back from me and studied it with a huge, self-satisfied grin on her face.

"When did you last see him?" I asked, checking his other favorite nap spots. Maybe the sun wasn't following its normal, predictable pattern today. Perhaps cloud cover had interfered. I knew my cat well enough to know he hadn't voluntarily changed his routine.

Something was off, and the sooner I figured out what that was, the better I'd feel going into the rest of the day.

Nan came over and gave my shoulder a little

squeeze. "I watched an episode of *Criminal Intent* with him during my mid-morning tea. That was only a little more than two hours ago. I'm sure he's fine, dear."

But I wasn't. Not at all.

I'd already lost him briefly a couple weeks ago, when he'd ended up on Caraway Island as if by magic. I still had no idea how he'd gotten out there or why I couldn't remember going with Nan to pick him up. All I knew is I needed to find my cat, and I needed to find him now.

"Help me look for him. Would you?" I asked Nan.

She nodded and tucked the metal sign away in the closet, then together we conducted a thorough search of both the house and the yard.

"Well, that's strange," Nan said, scratching her forehead. "Maybe he's just out for a walk and lost track of time."

Again, this was not how my cat operated. If I so much as tried to sleep in an extra minute, I'd get an earful about how disappointed he was in me. He did use his cat door as Nan suggested, but he never strayed far.

At least not until today.

A swatch of white appeared at the bottom of the

driveway, and I watched as the mail truck drew closer and closer.

"Beautiful day, isn't it?" the mail lady, Julie, trilled as she rummaged through her sack. "A light load today," she said next as she handed me a stack of mail that had been folded together using a thin rubber band.

"Thank you, Julie!" I called after her, biting my lip as I quickly flipped through the junk mail, bills, and solicitations.

But then I found an unfamiliar envelope, one that had no return address and was addressed simply to *"Octavius" Fulton*.

Yes, to my cat.

I swallowed hard and tore it open without even the slightest moment's hesitation...

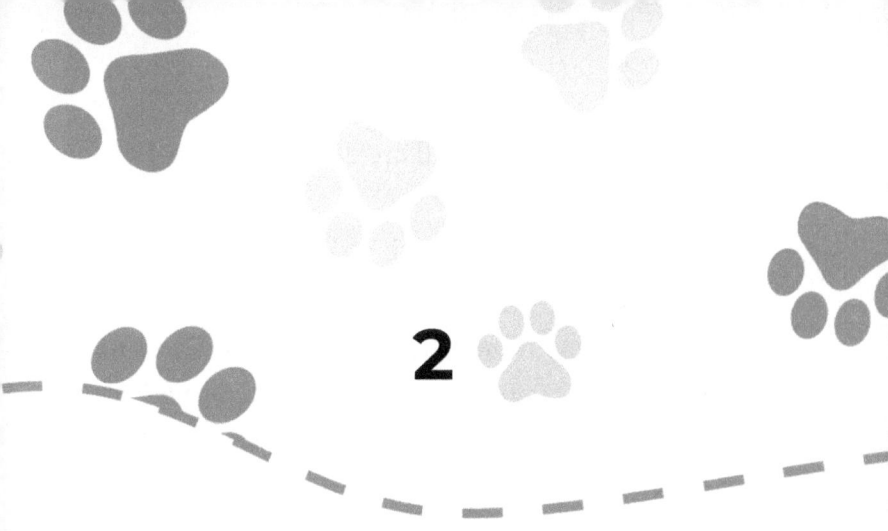

2

The date at the top of the letter had already passed two months ago. Not a good sign. Not good at all.

"What is it?" Nan asked as I quickly scanned the legalese before me.

"It's..." I took a deep, shaky breath in an effort to avoid either screaming or breaking down in tears. "It's an arbitration notice."

Nan's face loomed closer, concern pinching at the edges of her mouth. "An arbitration for what?" she huffed with clear outrage.

After a deep, painful swallow, I forced my eyes to focus on the page and read the entire letter from top to bottom before I spoke again. "The other beneficiaries of Ethel's will are disputing Octo-Cat's inheritance."

"Oh, dear," Nan said with a disappointed shake of her head.

"If he wants to contest, he has to appear in court by this Friday. Otherwise his agreement will be implied, and the arbitration will go forward." Even as I spoke the words, I couldn't quite believe them. Why was this happening now? Or ever for that matter? It's not like the others had gotten cut out of the will. Ethel had loved her cat dearly and wanted to make sure he lived the rest of his days comfortably. Knowing Octo-Cat as I did now, I totally understood. It wasn't exactly cheap to fulfill his demands for Fancy Feast, Evian, fine china, Apple products, and—oh—a giant East Coast manor house.

I folded the letter back into thirds and sighed, pinching the bridge of my nose to stave off the rapidly building headache. "Nan, if this goes forward, he could lose his trust fund. We could lose the house. We could even lose him."

I would not cry. Crying wouldn't fix this. It wouldn't bring Octo-Cat home. I needed to suck those tears that threatened to spill back in and approach both situations with a clear head.

Nan placed a hand at the small of my back and guided me back toward the house. "Well, we'll just have to find him by Friday, then," she ground out. "Failure is not an option."

My cat had only been missing for a few hours, tops, but already I was terrified for him. He'd be devastated if he lost his inheritance and I could no longer afford to maintain his lavish lifestyle and expensive tastes. Worse still was the fact that he could be lying hurt in a ditch somewhere, and I didn't even know where to look.

Nan motioned for me to sit on our massively uncomfortable antique Victorian couch. "You wait here while I make tea," she instructed softly. "The hit of caffeine will help wake up our brains. We'll solve this. Yes, we will." She hurried out of sight, singing to herself as she went.

That just left me sitting on my own in our large, empty living room. I hated it. Octo-Cat should have been there, complaining about something, questioning my life choices, or telling tasteless jokes that no one else found funny.

While I worked hard not to let fear cloud my normally rational brain, Nan continued to sing loudly from the kitchen. Apparently, she'd already composed a ballad about our mighty victory over catnappers and arbitrations. I had no idea where she found the energy.

Could a catnapper really be to blame for Octo-Cat's sudden disappearance? It was certainly a possibility, given how unlikely it would be for him to wander off on his own. But who would want to take my crabby tabby, and why?

Nan's gray, curly head popped out of the kitchen. "Yoo-hoo, Angie dear!" she called, waving at me.

I lifted my head and attempted a smile that wouldn't come.

"Why don't you give our good friend Charles a call? May as well update him on the situation and see if he can help." As soon as she'd said her piece, Nan disappeared from view and the singing started up again.

Charles. Would he know what to do? Nan seemed to think so, and the three of us had made a pretty good team more than once before. At the very least, he'd be able to walk me through this arbitration notice and help me formulate a plan for escaping unscathed.

The phone felt heavy in my hands. Placing this call meant admitting that something was wrong. That Octo-Cat was really missing. Could I maybe pretend for a few blessed minutes that everything was still okay? Would that be selfish of me? Stupid?

"Don't dilly-dally, dear!" Nan trilled from her place in front of the stove, then switched to singing in a different language. I assumed Korean, given her newly discovered K-pop infatuation.

Not even the deepest breath I could muster filled my lungs with the strength I needed to make this call, to speak these dreaded words aloud. But I did it anyway. I did it for Octo-Cat.

"Angie, everything okay?" Charles answered after a couple rings. He was still at the firm, of course. He'd been putting in long hours ever since Bethany had put in her resignation notice. With her moving away to start a new life in Georgia any day now, that left Charles as the sole partner at a law office that had seen a veritable revolving door of attorneys these past several months.

Hearing his voice so full of concern, of kind-ness, set off the tears I'd already been struggling to hold back. "Charles, he's gone!" I cried. "Octo-Cat is missing, and we can't find him anywhere."

Charles sucked in a deep breath, then said, "I'm sure he just found a great new napping spot and will wander home when his belly starts rumbling."

The way he rushed through this explanation

proved that Charles didn't believe those words. And neither did I. We both knew my cat too well to believe he had willingly altered his routine.

"There's also this arbitration thing," I added, knowing I should probably re-open the letter and read the exact wording. But I was already far too tired, too emotionally spent to read that horrible thing again.

"What?" Charles's voice came out low, hostile almost. "Who's requested an arbitration with you?"

"Not me," I corrected with another deep, weighty sigh. "Octo-Cat. And it's the other recipients of Ethel's will."

He was silent for a few moments as he contemplated this newest development in the everyday traumas of Angie Russo. "Don't let that add to your worry," he said at last. "For now, just focus on finding Octo-Cat. He can't be far. Besides, we both knew that the will would probably be contested eventually despite Richard's best attempts to prevent that from happening. You'll have a chance to contest the dispute before the arbitration goes ahead, too."

"Yeah, but the deadline's Friday," I said glumly. So far, I'd managed to avoid going to court for any personal matters. The only reason I'd ever stepped foot in the county court before was to offer on-the-spot assistance for the lawyers from my firm. Usually, Charles.

He balked at this. "Friday? But that's nowhere near enough time."

"Yeah, I know." I traced the intricate paisley pattern on the couch with my index finger, letting my vision go blurry but still refusing to let any tears fall. With a sniff, I informed Charles that, "The letter has a few different postmarks on it. Looks like it originally went to my old rental and then got turfed back as undeliverable until they finally found my forwarding address."

"But they all know exactly where you and Octo-Cat are," he protested. Charles had always been the sort to wear his heart right on his sleeve, and as such, I could tell that he'd become angry. *Real angry.*

I nodded, even though he wasn't there to read my body language. "I know that, too."

We both sighed in unison, and then I asked the question that had been plaguing me ever since the letter first arrived. "Do you think they sent it to the wrong place on purpose?"

"Of course I do," he growled. I could hear something slam down on his end of the line. "It's still okay. We'll find Octo-Cat in no time at all. Meanwhile I'll start putting together your grounds for contesting the arbitration, and we'll show up on Friday ready to kick some serious complainant butt."

"Thank you. You always make me feel better." That was Charles for you. He never hesitated to offer his help when I needed it, and that was a big part of the reason why he'd become my closest friend since he relocated from his home state of California in favor of the scenic Blueberry Bay region of Maine.

"Want me to stop by after work to help you look for Octo-Cat?" he asked me after a brief pause. "I could finish up early and offer a second set of eyes. Or third, rather, since I'm sure Nan's already on the case."

I let out a weak laugh. He knew us too well. "Actually, I kind of could use a change of scenery. We've already been searching for hours, and he's clearly nowhere nearby."

"Want to come over to my place, then?" he asked without even the briefest hesitation.

"Yes, please," I trilled.

Now that Charles was on the case, I knew everything would be okay. I had to believe that, because the alternative simply broke my heart.

If Octo-Cat were here, he'd no doubt yell at me to toughen up and do what needed to be done. And that's exactly what I would do to bring him back home—and to make sure we kept him here, right where he belonged.

3

harles invited me to come over for a quick dinner and epic brainstorming session at six thirty that evening. When I showed up at six thirty-three, however, the house stood dark and empty. Assuming he'd gotten delayed at work, I decided to let myself in using the key he kept stashed in the garden around back. At least it was a better hiding place than Nan's preferred placement under the front door mat. It's a wonder she never got burgled even once in all her seventy-ish years of life.

"Hello!" I called as I pushed my way inside, just in case Charles was in the shower or something and hadn't heard me knock.

Nothing.

I shrugged, then made my way to the kitchen. The least I could do is set the table, since I assumed he'd be bringing takeout home with him. Neither of us were great cooks, but thankfully I had my newly awakened culinary genius Nan to make sure I always had something yummy on my plate. It was both a blessing and a curse, considering I'd grown at least one pants size in the months since she'd discovered this new passion of hers.

I marched through the house, turning on some lights as I went, knowing Charles preferred to keep the curtains drawn for some odd reason. It still felt incredibly odd, though—seeing the house that I'd grown up in now set with all of Charles's sparse, manly decorations. Nan had decided to sell her former home and move in with me when I gained possession of the big manor house we both resided in now, which meant putting this one on the market.

It all worked out kind of perfect in the end, considering Charles needed something a bit more permanent than the Cliffside Apartments, where he used to live. Cliffside was also host to a vast percentage of Glendale's criminals—or, at least the ones that got caught. Based on my own unique experience as of late, the more money a person had, the more likely they were to kill somebody to protect it.

Some people were just never happy, and I vowed never to let myself become one of them.

Feeling a bit more at home now, I grabbed a pair of plates from the cupboard by the stove, then turned to head back out to the dining room and almost jumped right out of my skin at the horrifying sight before me.

"Oh my gosh," I cried, fumbling the plates in my shock, but thankfully not dropping them. "You scared me!"

Yes, it seemed I was no longer alone. Charles still hadn't put in an appearance, but his two Sphynx cats had appeared in the doorway and stood contemplating me with twin sets of glowing eyes. How had I forgotten about them?

"Hello, Jacques and Jillianne," I said with a friendly smile. Hopefully, they couldn't see that I was internally screaming at that moment. J and J, as Charles had taken to calling them whenever discussing the cats as a pair, had no hair but lots of wrinkles on their exposed skin. If you try to picture what a brain might look like if it grew four legs, a tail, and a pair of glowing eyes, then you'd have a pretty good idea why I was so startled at the initial sighting of these two.

The larger of the animals—Jillianne—stepped toward me. "A prince, a princess, and a paralegal walk into a kitchen. Which didn't belong?" she said, allowing me to hear one of the famous Sphynx cat riddles firsthand for the very first time. After all, it was only very recently I'd gained the ability to talk to anyone of fur or feather other than Octo-Cat.

Jillianne flicked her tail and narrowed her eyes when I didn't immediately answer. "Oh," I sputtered, suddenly feeling as if I were a contestant in the final round of Jeopardy—and that I'd just bid all my money without having the slightest idea what the answer might be. "Is the answer the paralegal? Um, because I'm here by Charles's invitation, I swear!"

I raised my hand and crossed my heart, hoping it would reassure the suspicious felines. It did not. Little Jacques arched his back and let out a dry, hacking hiss.

I took two giant steps back and put out my hands before me. "Don't you remember me? I took care of you, when..." Probably best not to bring up their recent trauma involving the untimely murder of their first owner. "I helped solve the case and get justice for the Senator. Remember?"

"Angie?" Charles's voice sounded from the other room followed by fast approaching footfalls. "Are you talking to J and J?" he asked when he'd made it to the kitchen. "I thought you couldn't do that."

Oh, crud.

I crossed my arms and scowled at him. "How is it that you are always the one to randomly discover all my secrets? Seriously, how?"

"Lucky timing?" he offered, lifting Jillianne into his arms and giving her a kiss on her forehead. And let me tell you, that cat went from threatening my life to contentedly purring within a matter of seconds.

I let out a giant, happy sigh. Well, at least I was safe now. I was also never going to let myself into Charles's house with the spare key ever again.

"So..." Charles said, drawing the single syllable into several long beats. His green eyes bore into me, and I found myself trapped in his gaze. "You can talk to all animals now? Because this development would have come in handy when we were working the Calhoun case."

"Shut up," I grumbled, trying and failing to

look away. Even when he was irritated with me, Charles's expression still held so much kindness. "You still won. And yes. I can talk to other animals now. I have no idea what changed or why, and I'd prefer to keep it hush-hush for now, please."

"Do you hear that?" he asked the black hairless cat in his arms using an adorable baby voice. "She thinks we're going to share her secret. Yes, she does."

It was strange how hot I found it watching Charles baby and dote on his creepy cat. Obviously, my crush was never going away, no matter how many times I accidentally walked in on him kissing his horrible girlfriend, Breanne. Regardless of his bad taste in... well, many things but especially girl-friends... Charles was the best guy I knew. Bar none.

He proved that further by coming in close and rubbing a calming hand on my shoulder. "We're going to find Octo-Cat, and we're going to dismiss this arbitration. Everything is going to be just fine."

The friction from his touch gave me a little thrill that I quickly worked to stuff down. He was my friend, my boss, the most inappropriate choice possible. Not for me, at least not right now.

I let out a weary sigh. It had been such a long day already.

Charles set Jillianne back onto the floor and searched my face for a moment. "You do believe me. Don't you?"

"Yes," I said without hesitation. Even though I didn't know what the future might one day hold for the two of us, I knew Charles would take care of everything going wrong in the present. I also knew that one way or another we would all be okay. Unfortunately, I didn't know what it might cost us in the meantime.

"What's the real pot of gold at the end of the rainbow?" the smaller spotted cat, Jacques, asked me from his spot on the kitchen floor. Apparently, he wasn't as good at riddles as his companion, which is why he typically let her speak for the both of them.

Still, I couldn't help but wonder what the answer to this one might be. Was it important? Would it somehow help me find my missing cat?

"Do you know what the pot of gold at the end of the rainbow really is?" I asked Charles as I rolled one of my hangnails beneath my thumb—a disgusting nervous habit I'd given up on trying to overcome.

He blinked at me a few times, then burst out laughing. "I don't know. A bowl of cereal. Weird question."

I looked back toward Jacques, but he'd retreated back into the bowels of the house. Was he just messing with me, or had he tried to share something important?

Perhaps I'd never know.

4

"I hope you're in the mood for some fried chicken," Charles said at the same moment I spotted the red-and-white containers stacked in the center of the table. "It seemed comfort food-y," he added with a grin as the two of us moved into the dining room.

"It smells so good," I cooed. Then I remembered the one time I'd attempted to bring fast food chicken into the house while living with Octo-Cat. He'd claimed the greasy smell bothered him so much that he'd swatted the still-full bucket off the edge of the table, sending wings, thighs, and drumsticks cascading across the dusty floor and rendering my dinner plans obsolete.

That guy. He always did love making a scene.

Charles studied me carefully as he scooped a giant heap of mashed potatoes onto his plate. "What's up?" he asked softly.

"Just thinking about him," I admitted, returning to that sad, anxiety-filled place inside of me. "Do you really think he's okay?"

"Angie, look at me," Charles demanded, his stern expression brooking no argument. "That cat of yours could probably survive a nuclear holocaust if he wanted to. You know, he's kind of like a cockroach in that way. Nothing stands in the way of him and what he wants, and I guarantee he wants to get home to you. And he will. Okay?"

"Okay," I mumbled. Should I be offended that he basically just called my cat a cockroach? Octo-Cat certainly wouldn't like that comparison if he were here. But he wasn't here, and I was beginning to worry we'd never find him—especially not in time to make his court date.

Charles gave me a few minutes alone with my thoughts, but the whole time his gaze didn't waver from my face. "Tell me you believe me," he said at last.

"Yes, yes, I believe you," I hurried to assure him. In some ways I did, but in others? It was hard to keep the faith when I had no idea what we were dealing with. "It's still hard, though," I added, unable to hide the emotional turmoil that raged on the inside. Had I somehow caused this? If so, I would never forgive myself.

"Eat," Charles commanded, motioning to my plate, where the salty pile of comfort food still sat untouched.

Even though I knew Charles was just trying to help, my stomach churned at the sight of it. I twisted my face into a grimace and leaned away from the table, trying to gain at least a little distance from the nauseating aroma before me.

My thoughts immediately turned back to Octo-Cat. "Do you think he has access to Evian and Fancy Feast wherever he is? What if he's starving or dying of thirst? What if—?"

"Okay, that's it," Charles said firmly as he set his fork down and pushed his plate to the side. "You're officially not allowed to talk until you get something in your stomach."

"But—" I argued, unsure of how I wanted to finish this particular sentence. Luckily, I didn't have to.

"But nothing," Charles huffed, folding his arms in front of him. "While you eat, I'll do the talking. Got it?"

I sat, staring at him with a furrowed brow, which elicited a deep sigh from Charles.

Both his voice and expression softened then. "C'mon. I'm trying to be a good friend here."

Even though my gut still roiled with anxiety, I obediently picked up a chicken leg and smiled at Charles with wide eyes before taking a large, juicy bite. Instead of feeling worse like I'd feared, something like relief settled over me. Maybe I really was hungry, after all.

"Thank you," he said with a quick nod in my direction. "Now, we have a couple of big issues to address. Let's start with the arbitration, because I'm assuming it will be easier for you to focus on your dinner while I'm yammering on about the boring stuff."

I gave him a thumbs up and waited to see what he'd say next.

"Like I said before, we should have Octo-Cat back by then, which means it probably won't be a problem for us." He held up his hand to silence me before I could even begin to offer another argument.

"However," he continued emphatically. "Just to make sure all our bases are covered, I'll stop by the county court tomorrow to request a continuance.

Meanwhile, I shouldn't need much to prepare your argument against the arbitration. Ethel Fulton made her will very clear in regard to how she wanted her assets divided and who she most wanted to see benefited by them. And while she was certainly the most generous with Octo-Cat, she didn't cut any of the family out, either."

He paused to take a quick drink from his glass of tap water. Funny how my cat had more particular tastes than the senior partner at my law firm. "Now, they might argue that Octo-Cat and his monthly trust fund payments should have remained with one of the members of their family, but that won't be a problem, either. We have lots of evidence that you're a fantastic pet owner. Many witnesses who would attest to that fact as well."

I pushed my plate aside, already having eaten all I could stomach for the time being. I did feel better in some ways, but in others nothing had changed. And now my head swam with all the new information Charles had provided about how we were going to fight this arbitration.

"Well, maybe I *was* a fantastic pet owner," I murmured with a frown. "But now my pet either ran away or was stolen right out from under my nose."

Charles waved his fork at me, sending a small lump of mashed potatoes soaring half way across the table. We both stared at the spot where they'd landed for a moment without saying anything.

"We're going to find him," he promised again. "And you know how you're going to do it, right?"

I lifted my eyes to his with what I assume must have appeared to be a blank expression, when inside my head was reeling with all the places we had yet to look, all the things that might have possibly gone wrong in the meanwhile.

"Um, hello!" he cried, waving his hand between us with a flourish. "You can talk to other animals now. That's huge!"

"J and J weren't exactly thrilled to see me," I hedged. Even though I could talk to other animals, I hadn't done much of that yet. I was still learning, and there was so much I needed to figure out, given that each species seemed to have its own personality, lingo, and set of social guidelines. Heck, I was still figuring out Octo-Cat more and more with each new day, and now I had an entire world of creatures I knew very little about. It wasn't as if I had anyone I could ask for advice on this particular issue, either.

"Not them," Charles said with a dismissive

chuckle, referring to his two moody felines. "I'm sure there are at least a dozen forest animals that regularly hang out in your yard or in the woods by your yard. Maybe one of them saw something."

"Oh my gosh, you're right," I said, suddenly eager to get home again. Even if I didn't know exactly how to act with them, at least I had my words. At this point I'd try anything—risk almost everything—to find my missing friend again.

Charles simpered at me. "Do you feel better now?"

I knew I wouldn't feel better until I had Octo-Cat safe in my arms again. Granted, he would probably scratch me like crazy, considering how hard I planned to hug his furry little body once I found him again. Even the sting a of fresh wound would be welcome right about now. Anything to prove that my cat was still here and that he didn't blame me for his sudden disappearance.

Actually, even if he did blame me, that would still be okay. I'd have to work harder to make sure nothing like this ever happened again.

"Thanks for talking me off the ledge," I said as Charles began to clear our plates from the table.

"No more ledges for you," he said with a laugh. "You hear me?"

I knew he was just joking, but still I couldn't promise anything. If Octo-Cat needed me to walk a tightrope a hundred feet off the ground, I would jump at the chance to do it.

Anything to bring my number one guy home safe and sound...

5

Nan was nowhere to be found when I returned home from Charles's place. Her little red sports coupe was missing, too, which led me to assume she was out widening our search radius.

Now that the twilight hour had set in, the animals who normally scampered and flittered around my yard had all tucked in for the night. Some of the forest creatures were most definitely nocturnal, but I felt uneasy going into the dark woods without backup. Instead, as much as it pained me, I decided to head to bed early so that I could also wake up early to resume my search.

"Wherever you are," I whispered, hoping somehow, some way Octo-Cat would hear or would at least know I was thinking of him, "I hope you're okay."

The next morning, I dragged myself out of bed at the first sign of dawn. The animals were up, and I needed to be as well. Nan's little red sports coupe was back in front of the house, but she herself wasn't up yet. She had, however, left a long and very detailed note for me on the kitchen counter:

My dearest dear,

I know you are eager to find our missing buddy, but make sure you grab a bite to eat first. Scones are in the ceramic container on the opposite side of the fridge. I also brought home some of those cold coffees that taste like chalk in case I'm not up early enough to make the brew.

As for the search, here are all the places I checked last night...

What followed was a lengthy list of almost every place in Glendale. No wonder Nan was still in bed. She must have been out all night. Yet still, she hadn't managed to find "our missing buddy." More and more it was looking like foul play had been involved, and that made finding him all the more urgent. I grabbed one of Nan's scones and a chilled coffee shot from the fridge, planning to eat while I searched the woods.

Or rather *interrogated* the local woodland creatures.

Outside, the sun was bright and warm like a reassuring hug. Hopefully, the animals would be every bit as accommodating as the weather.

Then we might really get somewhere.

A little chickadee sat on the porch railing, tilting its head to the side as it studied me.

I stopped in my tracks and plastered on my best smile. "Hello, there," I said around a very full mouth of scone.

The short, fat bird quickly became a tall, thin bird as it rose on its tiptoes and stretched its neck high in alarm. "It speaks!" he cried.

I nodded and swallowed down my food before speaking again. "My name's Angie, and I was wondering if you could help me with—" My words fell away once the chickadee flapped its wings furiously and darted away without so much as a backward glance in my direction.

Well, then. It seemed clear I would need to find something a little less skittish than a bird. I already knew from my limited experience that almost everything seemed to set them off and send them flying away. Definitely not the most useful as far as witnesses went.

Leaving the porch behind, I made my way toward the edge of the forest that edged my property on three sides. Once there, I stood stock-still and listened to the morning chorus all around me. Much of it belonged to a cacophony of various birds singing in the trees, but I'd already decided that I'd only be questioning them as an absolute last resort.

A chittering sound came from above, and sure enough a hyper brown squirrel jumped from one branch to the next, singing a peppy little tune that seemed to be about all his favorite kinds of nuts.

"Oh, what a beautiful day for eating an acorn," he belted out, then hummed a few beats before continuing his song. "Hey, it's always a great day to enjoy a walnut!"

"Hey!" I called in his general direction. I didn't know much about squirrels, but they definitely didn't seem to be the shyest of creatures. Perhaps I could use that to my advantage now.

The squirrel immediately stopped singing, stopped moving, stopped everything as he took me in with his shiny, black eyes.

"I heard you like nuts," I said, formulating my plan right there on the spot. "But do you like peanut butter?"

He sniffed the air with giant, exaggerated motions. It practically looked as if his nose would fly straight off his face. A second later, he zagged to the side and scampered down to the base of the tree. "Do-do-do you have peanut butter?"

"That depends." I crossed my arms and tried to appear to look both bored and non-threatening.

Luckily, Mr. Squirrel wasn't up on the latest human bribery techniques, because my hesitation to answer his question only made his eagerness grow. "You dooooo have peanut butter. Don't you?" He closed about half the distance between us and sniffed at the air again.

"My name's Angie. I live in that house back there," I informed him, hooking a thumb over my shoulder in the general direction of the manor house.

The fuzzy rodent before me nodded vigorously. "I'm Maple. I live about three trees back and five to the right." Now that part of the squirrel's energy was being used to nod, its voice came out squeakier but also less hurried. Different. This was the point that I realized Maple was most likely actually a girl.

I didn't know how to politely ask, so I just did my best to avoid any gendered language as our conversation proceeded. "I'm trying to find my friend," I explained. "If you can help me with that, then there's a whole jar of peanut butter in it for you."

Maple's eyes grew even wider as she scrambled straight up to me and put both of her furry little hands on the toe of my shoe. "Really? A whole jar?" she asked almost reverently, unwilling to take her eyes off me for even a second.

"Yup," I confirmed with an earnest smile. "But I need help figuring out where my friend's gone first."

"Do you mean the other human? Or maybe the cat?" Maple reached one small hand up and scratched at her head. "I don't think there's anyone else in your drey is there?"

"The cat," I said with a nod. "And how do you

know so much about my... drey?" I stumbled over the unfamiliar word, assuming this must be what a squirrel called its family.

"I like to watch you sometimes from my tree," Maple answered unabashedly. "Sometimes I even climb up onto the roof to get a closer look. You're a funny trio, you three are."

I couldn't tell whether that was meant as an insult or some kind of strange compliment, so I just said, "Um, thank you?" It was a bit creepy that Maple had made a habit of peeping in on us, but I tried to let that go—especially if it led to information we could use to recover Octo-Cat.

"You are very welcome," the squirrel said, sniffing at the air yet again. "Peanut butter?"

"First cat, then peanut butter," I reminded her.

"Oh, I'm so hungry, just thinking about all that gooey, melty nut butter, but I promise I will try my very best to help!"

Clearly, it was going to be difficult to keep my new squirrel friend on task, so I'd need to be quick and to the point with my questions. First, I needed to give her a little background on the situation.

"Octo-Cat went missing yesterday during the late morning or very early afternoon," I explained.

"We've been looking everywhere but haven't been able to find him. We're wondering if maybe someone took him. Did you see anything unusual happening around here at that time?"

"Unusual? Hmmm." Maple grabbed her tail and began to brush through it with her fingers. Her eyes darted from side to side as she thought. "The big buck was here. You know the one with lots of pointy parts on his antlers? He was hanging out near the edge of the forest, which I thought was weird since he usually likes to stay hidden. And my friend, Willow, said she saw the old human taking a nap in the sun."

"Nan?" That definitely didn't sound like my active, vibrant grandmother, but who else could it be?

"Sure, I guess so." Maple put her hands out to either side in an approximation of a shrug. "I don't blame him, since sleeping in the sunshine is so nice. The only thing nicer is nuts—especially peanut butter. Do you still have some you wanted to give me?"

"Nan's a she, by the way," I said with a small chuckle. "Don't worry about it, though. I know it can be hard to tell with humans. And, yes, I have that jar of peanut butter I promised you. But do you think maybe you can help me out with something very important, Maple?"

She spun in a slow circle, searching the woods around us. I looked, too, but didn't see or hear any other animals nearby.

Maple turned back toward me with her mouth ajar. "Didn't I do that already?"

I had to make fast on my peanut butter promise. Otherwise I'd lose the opportunity to get anything else from my first animal informant. "Yes, which is why I'm giving you the first jar of peanut butter. I'll give you another if you can ask around the forest and see if you can learn anything—anything at all —about what might have happened to my cat."

Maple saluted me, then ran off shouting into the forest. No idea where she learned that partic- ular gesture or how screaming to all the animals at once was going to help anything, but I could at least keep up my end of the promise.

Now I knew that at least some of the animals kept a close eye on my house and family. Did that mean one of them saw what happened yesterday?

I returned home to raid my pantry for a fresh jar of peanut butter, hoping that when I returned, Maple might have more to tell me.

Each moment that passed by without my cat's safe return had become agonizing for me, and I wasn't sure I could last another night without knowing he was safe.

Oh, Octo-Cat, where have you gone?

6

Even though I'd barely been out for half an hour, I returned home to find Nan both wide awake and wearing a full face of makeup. She also wore a lace-trimmed blue sundress that hit at the knees, which she'd paired with hot pink tights and big dangling earrings.

"Hey, good morning. What are you all dressed up for?" I asked, eyeing her suspiciously as I clicked the door shut behind me.

"Dressed up?" Nan asked with a small frown as she scratched at her collarbone. "Are you sure? I was worried it makes me look too much like an old fogey."

I widened my eyes and shook my head. Nothing about Nan's ensemble aged her in the slightest, but

I also knew better than to argue with her when it came to fashion. We both had a special flair for it but tended to prefer very different styles.

"The lace, dear," Nan explained. "Doesn't it feel a bit old-fashioned to you?"

"I think you look nice," I offered with a smile and shrug as I sat to join her. "But I still don't know why you're all dressed up."

"Oh, yes. Well, that nice young man, Brock, called and said he was coming by to do a bit of work." Nan shimmied her shoulders and giggled—actually giggled.

This was weird. Even for her.

And especially for so early in the morning.

"He prefers to be called Cal now," I pointed out. "You know, short for Calhoun."

Nan studied her reflection in the antique mirror that hung near the doorway. "Ah, so he does."

"But none of this explains why you felt the need to dress all..." I stopped just short of saying *flirty* and let out a big gasp. *Of course.* "Nan, you don't have a new crush, do you?"

She waved her hand and rolled her eyes, but the blush that now painted the apples of her cheeks was unmistakable. "Oh, pish posh. I don't think it can be categorized as a crush if I never plan on making a move. Besides, silly, I've already decided he's for you."

"For me?" I shrieked. "You can't be serious!"

"He's single. You're single. You get along. I don't see what the problem is..." A wicked smile lit up her face. "Unless you have romantic inclinations for another fella?"

Sure, there was no denying that Cal was an attractive man and somebody I got along well with, too. But to think about dating at a time like this? No way. Not until Octo-Cat was back home, safe and sound.

I groaned and cracked my neck to either side. "This is not the 1800s, nor is it the Deep South. We live in twenty-first-century Maine, Nan. And I can find my own boyfriend when I'm ready. Right now, I'm a bit more concerned about finding my missing cat, thank you."

Nan remained completely unperturbed by my protestations. "Still no reason to pass up a perfectly good opportunity when it just so happens to present itself," she said. "Besides, you say you can find your own boyfriend, but you haven't. Let your poor old nan help. By the way, is that what you're planning to wear?"

"That's it!" I shouted, throwing both hands in

the air and marching right past her. "I'll meet Cal outside, and you can make yourself scarce. Preferably by continuing the search for Octo-Cat." Even though I knew it was a touch overdramatic, I slammed the door shut behind me and practically ran straight into the handsome handyman on the other side.

"Oh, sorry," I murmured as I tried to edge my way past him without losing my footing or brushing up against anything I shouldn't. I found myself even more aware of his good looks than normal now, thanks to Nan.

Cal's brow furrowed in sympathy. "Is everything okay?"

"Just peachy," I said, giving a thumbs-up and tossing him a wink for good measure. Ugh. Why was I always embarrassing myself?

Cal stretched his hand across the back of his neck and glanced down toward the porch. "Your nan called me a little bit ago and said you needed help installing a sign for your new business." He glanced up again and his dark eyes locked with mine. "I didn't know you were starting up your own business. If you need any advice or anything, I'd be happy to help in whatever way I can."

Nan had said Cal called himself, but seeing as

he had no reason to lie about things, I had to wonder why Nan would have intentionally misled me. What was she playing at, and why now?

"Thanks, Cal. That's…" I stopped and cleared my throat, otherwise it felt like I might legitimately stop breathing. "That's really nice of you. I'll definitely let you know if I need any help."

He rocked back and forth on the balls of his feet and glanced awkwardly toward the door before finally asking, "So, um, where's the sign?"

"Oh, just a sec. I'll go in and grab it real quick. Be right back." I raced inside, clicking the door shut behind me so that Cal wouldn't try to follow. The last thing I needed was an added layer of embarrassment from Nan. I was doing a mighty fine job of that myself, thank you. I grabbed the metal sign and stepped back outside, where I handed it to Cal.

He laughed as he studied it. "I'm guessing your nan made this."

"Yup." I stared at the door, praying that Nan wasn't planning on bursting through it anytime soon.

"So you're opening a… what exactly?"

"A private investigation firm." I bit my lip while he continued to stare at the sign with a furrowed brow.

"And you're a pet whisperer now?" His eyes snapped up and locked with mine.

I took a step back and forced a laugh. "It's just a cute name Nan and my mom came up with."

"So you don't talk to animals?" he asked, raising an eyebrow now. He didn't appear judgmental, just curious. Still. I really would have preferred a different name for my new firm.

I shook my head so hard, I practically got whiplash. "No, ha! Don't be silly!"

"Too bad," Cal said after making a gentle clicking noise with his tongue. "I think it would be interesting to hear what they had to say."

"Yeah," I said with a laugh. "I'm sure it would be. Especially considering my cat turned up missing yesterday, and I'm worried sick about him."

"Octavius, right?" he asked. "I remember that guy. Do you need any help searching for him? It should only take me a few minutes to hang this sign, and then I have the rest of the day free."

I took a deep breath, suddenly feeling much better about Cal's visit. Nan was only trying to help expand our search team. All the flirty stuff was just her way of adding a bit of dramatic flair, but not really the point. "Thank you, Brock—I mean, Cal.

That would be really nice, if you're sure you don't mind."

A curtain rustled in the window, and I saw Nan poke her head into view wearing a giant, naughty grin. I, of course, shot her a death glare. Whether or not her heart was in the right place, sometimes her tongue ran away with her. Sometimes I needed to put my foot down, to remind her that meddling with my life wasn't an appropriate—or appreciated—hobby.

Less than a minute later, Nan flung the front door open and pushed her way between us on the porch. "Did I hear you're going to help us search for our sweet missing kitty?" she cooed, batting eyelashes so long I had to wonder if she'd applied fake lashes—or at least several extra coats of mascara.

"Yes, of course," Cal answered, fixing her with a charming smile. I don't think I'd ever met a single person who didn't immediately adore my nan. It was kind of like her own personal superpower.

"Oh, goodie," she cried. "Angie and I need all the help we can get. We are so worried about our little guy."

"Think nothing of it. It's my pleasure," Cal assured us both just as another vehicle pulled up the driveway and stopped in front of our manor house.

Well, Nan and I were certainly popular this morning. I, of course, recognized the dusty black sedan right away. Sure enough, Charles parked quickly and then hurried over to join us on the porch.

"Nan," he cried. "I came as soon as I got your text. Is everything okay?"

Nan floated over to give him a hug hello, smiling at me as she did. Would every eligible bachelor in Blueberry Bay show up at my house this morning? Ugh, I sure hoped not.

Exactly two thoughts flittered through my mind then as the four of us stood awkwardly together on the porch.

One, I definitely regretted teaching my grandmother how to text.

And two, I was going to kill her.

7

Everyone except for Nan seemed a bit uncomfortable during our impromptu porch meeting. This was made incredibly clear by the fact that no one said anything for several moments.

"Are you okay?" Charles finally asked Nan again, seeing as she hadn't given him a clear answer upon his arrival. "Your text worried me."

"Oh. I'm fine, dear," she responded with a grandmotherly grin. "I'm just so worried about Octo-Cat. You know how it is. He didn't come home last night, and poor Angie is sick with worry, too. We could both really use some help and a friend through this trying time."

Well, that at least was true. I pumped my head

in agreement. "Sorry to call you out of work," I muttered by way of apology.

"That's okay," Charles said, placing a hand on my shoulder and giving it a quick squeeze. "This is important."

Cal shifted his weight between his feet and took a small step back. "Hi, Charles," he muttered.

"Brock," the other man said, clamping a hand on his shoulder now, too. "Good to see you, man."

Things seemed more than a little awkward between them, despite the fact that Charles had gotten Cal acquitted of a double murder charge not too long ago and had been dating Cal's twin sister for the past several months to boot.

Was the sister thing what made them so tense around each other? And if so, might that mean trouble in paradise? Most importantly, though, why was I so darned happy about that possibility? I needed to quit daydreaming and get back to focusing on finding my lost fur friend.

"I do have a bit of bad news, unfortunately," Charles said just then, looking from me to Nan and back again. "I exchanged some emails first thing this morning, and needless to say, we can't get a continuance for the arbitration."

"Which means?" Nan prompted as she rolled her hand at the wrist impatiently.

Charles sighed. "We need to find Octo-Cat and find him fast. That's the only way we'll be able to contest, and believe me, you'll want to contest."

"Wait," Cal said as he lifted his hands in apparent confusion. "The cat is the one who needs to go to court. Not the two of you?"

"The cat," Charles informed him, "is the beneficiary, so yes, he does need to be present."

Cal grabbed my hand and gave it a friendly squeeze, then said, "Don't worry, Angie. I'm sure we'll find him today, and if we don't, how hard could it be to find a lookalike to take to court in a pinch?"

My jaw dropped open, and I was too agitated to speak. I wanted to rip my hand away from anyone who would suggest such an awful solution to our problems.

Then Cal burst out laughing. "Sorry, just trying to lighten the mood with a bit of humor. I guess that joke flopped and flopped bad."

"It was a big ol' belly flop," Nan told him with a wink. "Why don't you come with me, Cal? We can buddy up for the search. Charles, are you fine escorting Angie?"

I saved my breath rather than try to explain to Nan that I didn't need an escort for this—or really anything else. It would be nice to spend some time with Charles, to have a partner in the search, especially since I was now losing hope at a depressingly rapid clip.

"We can pick up where we left off last night, or at least by doing what we talked about. Come with me," Charles said, motioning for me to follow him toward the woods.

The woods!

"Just a second," I called, darting back into the house and straight past Nan and Cal as I dashed toward the pantry. I found an unopened jar of peanut butter and grabbed it for my new squirrel informant, Maple, making sure to hide it from view as I passed Cal. No need to invite any awkward questions if they could just as easily be avoided.

"Have a craving?" Charles asked with a sarcastic smile when I returned to him.

Heat flooded my cheeks, but then I remembered that Charles knew everything, and I had absolutely nothing to be embarrassed about. "Let's just say I owe a squirrel a favor," I said, making a clicking noise as we fell into step beside one another.

"A squirrel, huh? Did he have any good leads for

you?" He asked this as if it were a completely normal and rational development, and I loved him for it.

"*She,* and not really. But I've asked her to be my eyes and ears in the forest, provided she stops thinking about peanut butter long enough to pay attention to anything else."

Charles chuckled. "Maybe we need to find you a different animal helper. Who do you think would be good at playing detective?" He raised his hand to his chin and rubbed it while making a funny face. He even took on a fake British accent as he ran through the possibilities.

"How about a bird, darling? Or a deer, my dear? Ooh, maybe a mountain lion!" He lost his phony accent on that last one, but I was still ridiculously charmed by him.

"Ha, ha," I said, willing my heart to stop beating so hard against my rib cage.

Charles bumped his shoulder into mine and sent that poor, overworked organ of mine galloping off at full speed again. "No, really. Who should we be looking for?"

"Well, the birds won't talk to me. Way too skittish," I informed him, still very much aware of how closely we walked beside each other. "I'm not sure what else is in the forest, and I've never talked to any of them before, so I just really don't know."

"C'mon," he said, extending his hand to me as we reached the edge of the tree line. "Let's go find out."

My pulse quickened as I took his hand. I knew he was just being gentlemanly, but at the same time, I'd been carrying a bit of a torch for the guy for the past several months. He didn't seem to have the slightest clue I felt how I did, given that he had a girlfriend and I was the one with the ace sleuthing skills.

But still. Still! My heart whomped wildly as I searched the trees and ground for any animal who might be willing to talk to us.

"Let's go deeper," Charles said, tugging me along.

"I've heard there are bears here if we go deep enough." A shiver ran through me as I imagined coming face-to-face with the most fearsome predator in all of Blueberry Bay. For some reason, bears didn't strike me as the type to talk through their problems—especially not with a meddlesome human such as myself.

"I ain't afraid of no bears," Charles said in a

sing-song voice. "Boy Scouts taught me how to take care of that."

I couldn't hold back the laugh that bubbled to the surface. "Ran into lots of bears in California, did you?"

"Tons," he confirmed, giving my hand a quick, playful squeeze.

A twig snapped several feet away, and our eyes both zoomed to the location. A light brown doe stood ramrod straight and perfectly still, her dark eyes boring into mine. I could feel her fear, sense the internal debate that raged within her as she tried to decide whether it would be better to stay frozen or make a run for it.

"We're not going to hurt you," I whispered evenly, but that was enough to send her zigzagging through the trees and out of our view.

"I won't hurt you!" I yelled after her. "I won't hurt any of you. Please won't somebody talk to me?"

Another twig snapped nearby. The leaves rustled under the weight of some kind of creature approaching us quickly from behind.

Charles stretched his arms out and blocked me with his body in a move so sudden it almost seemed as if he hadn't needed to think about it at all.

"Are you sure you're not afraid of bears?" I asked, trying to lighten the mood even though I was still more than a little frightened myself. I'd been caught off guard in these woods before, and a strange man had grabbed hold of my arms and covered my mouth. Obviously, I'd lived to tell the tale, but I didn't trust my chances if Charles and I really did run into the infamous Blueberry Bay bears.

Everything fell quiet.

Charles and I both waited in silence.

And then a blur of brown burst into view.

"Is that my peanut butter?" Maple squeaked, jumping from tree to tree in excitement and leaving me to wonder how one little squirrel had managed to make so much noise.

"Yes, it's yours," I said, squatting down to offer the jar. "But first I want to know what you found out for me."

Maple bolted toward me, stopping just short of my knees. "About what?"

"Um. About my missing cat?"

"Your cat is missing. Oh, no!"

I hoped squirrels weren't good at reading human emotions, because my disappointment was most definitely evident in that moment. Had Maple really forgotten everything we'd talked about already?

"Here," I said with a sigh as I unscrewed the cap of the peanut butter and handed the jar to the forgetful little squirrel. "Take it. It's yours."

Charles and I both watched as Maple pushed the peanut butter onto its side and rolled it away with a series of euphoric squeaks and shouts.

"C'mon," I said. "I don't think we're going to find what we're looking for out here."

I hated to admit defeat, but I also hated wasting time when Octo-Cat needed me. What was the point of explaining the situation to Maple when she would just forget again the second we said goodbye?

Maybe I should try to find that buck. If it meant getting my cat back, then it would be worth the risk...

8

"Back so soon?" Nan asked when Charles and I trudged into the house an hour after departing. Even our brief outing, however, had seemed to take forever. Charles had insisted we give our forest investigation a solid effort before calling it a total bust. But even he could see we weren't making any progress, despite the fact he couldn't talk with the animals himself.

"Yeah," I grumbled, kicking my shoes off by the door. "We accomplished absolutely nothing. How'd you guys fare?"

"I sent Cal home," Nan said with a dramatic sigh, anger flitting across her normally controlled features. "He lost at least ten points in my book when he suggested we find an Octo-doppelgänger. Talk about a terrible idea!"

Well, I couldn't disagree with her there. Joke or not, what Cal had said hurt us both, and it would have enraged Octo-Cat had he been around to hear it.

Nan now sat alone in the living room with a giant sheet of poster board sprawled across the floor in front of her. A row of colorful Sharpie markers lay nearby, and she clutched an angry-looking red one tightly in her hand.

"What are you doing?" Charles asked, moving in for a closer look.

"And where did you get all these crafting supplies?" I added as I trudged along after him.

Nan kept her attention on the spread before her as she explained, "I always keep a stash nearby. You never know when you're going to need to papier-mâché or pottery wheel your way out of a disaster."

"Oh, yeah. Well, of course," I said, making sure Charles caught my giant eyeroll. I loved Nan dearly, but sometimes her priorities seemed a bit out of whack—like deciding to play matchmaker when we had a missing cat to find.

She lowered the marker to the bright yellow

poster board and began to write while she mumbled, "I'm gathering all the facts we have so far in one place and all our suspicions, too. Consider this poster board command central. Now, look here. Red is for the things we know for sure. Blue is for the things we aren't quite sure of yet."

"And black?" Charles asked as he reached for the last marker.

"Black are ideas we've already eliminated. Things we know for sure aren't true," Nan said, bobbing her head as she continued to write in large, looping letters, then stopped to yank the Sharpie away from Charles. "That's mine, thank you very much."

"Nan..." I warned. Even though she had raised me, sometimes I felt like the mom in our relationship.

Charles just laughed it off. When he'd finished, we both stood in silence watching as Nan completed her project.

"Okay, kids. It's time to get serious here," Nan said a few minutes later after she'd finished making her list and recapped the final marker.

"What do we know so far?" I asked. The poster board had remained depressingly light on text, showing just how far we had yet to go.

Nan straightened up tall and folded her hands in her lap. "Octo-Cat is missing. *Fact,*" she began. "He disappeared between the hours of ten and one yesterday. *Fact.* He may have been taken against his will. *Suspicion.* A letter also arrived yesterday announcing the arbitration thingy. *Fact.* It could be related. *Suspicion.*"

"I don't see any black," I said, doing my best to read Nan's teeny tiny handwriting on the bright poster board but coming up short. "What have we been able to rule out?"

"Nothing yet," she announced with a frown. She spun the black marker between her fingers, and I could tell she desperately wanted to use it for something.

"Chin up," Charles said, gracing us both with a mega-watt albeit super-fake smile. "We're making progress. Even if it feels slow."

"Oh, let's make a list of all the places we've checked," Nan shouted with glee and began to push herself up off the floor.

I placed a hand on her shoulder and shook my head. "You already gave that to me this morning with your note. Remember?"

"Yes, but it's not on the poster board with all the other case info yet," she moaned.

"Hang tight. I'll go get it for you." I decided to just go with whatever Nan wanted in this case. At least she was getting us organized. All I'd done so far was go in circles around the forest, making myself both dizzy and frustrated in the process. I was also down one jar of peanut butter.

After retrieving the note from the kitchen, I read Nan the list of places she'd checked last night. She chose a green marker to note the places we'd already explored. Finally, the poster board began to look a little fuller, although I suppose that wasn't exactly a good thing. It meant we were running out of options.

"We'll find him," Charles assured everyone for what felt like the hundredth time that morning, and while I appreciated his optimism, I also kind of wished he'd just keep quiet already.

"Did you ask the neighbors?" he asked us.

Nan clucked her tongue. "Of course we asked the neighbors. That was the first thing we did yesterday afternoon."

"Well, what about—?" Charles began, but was cut off by the unexpected buzz of our electronic cat door lifting open in the nearby foyer.

Could it really be? Had he come home all on his own?

"Octo-Cat!" I cried, pushing myself to my feet and stumbling as fast as I could toward the door. His cat door had been programmed to open whenever it sensed the little chip on his collar, which meant it could only be Octo-Cat trotting through the door now. I began to cry softly as tears of relief pricked at my eyes.

Maybe he had just stayed out too late, or perhaps he'd strayed too far and then had a hard time finding home again. Oh, he had some major explaining to do, that kitty boy of mine.

I thrust a hand on my hip as I took the last few steps toward the door, ready to go full-on angry pet parent on his furry behind.

I turned the corner, and sure enough, the first thing I saw was that familiar striped tail of his. It seemed puffier than usual, which meant that he was also upset and scared.

Next I spotted a pair of fat gray haunches, which definitely did not match my brown tabby's fur. That's when I realized it wasn't Octo-Cat making his triumphant return. No. Instead, we had an imposter.

But how? How could it have possibly gotten inside without the special collar that interfaced with the pet door?

I was still puzzling over this when the creature turned around and stared at me from deep, masked eyes. A raccoon!

In one hand, he held Octo-Cat's broken collar and in the other an empty can of Fancy Feast. Where had this intruder come from, and why did he have my cat's things?

"You have some serious explaining to do!" I shouted, realizing too late that my anger may cause him to flee. Despite my anger and fear in that moment, this raccoon was our best lead. I had to play nice, even though I wanted to keep screaming until I got the answers I craved.

The raccoon wasn't afraid of me in the slightest. He held tight to both items and then stood on his hind legs, tilting his head to the side as he studied me. "Did you just talk?" he asked with a quizzical expression.

A brief moment of silence passed between us. I could feel Nan and Charles at my back, but neither said anything as the three of us stared the trespasser down.

Suddenly, our raccoon visitor burst out laughing in a high-pitched, squeaky giggle that immediately grated on my nerves. "Aww, you can talk! That's so cute!"

I hated to think what might have happened next had Nan and Charles not each grabbed one of my arms and held me back. It would have been a very low moment, indeed, if I'd gotten into a fight with a raccoon—especially since I was pretty sure that I would have lost.

rounded on the beady-eyed intruder. Perhaps I should have been afraid of rabies or some other random infection, but in that moment I was just too angry to care about anything other than finding some answers. "Why do you have my cat's collar?" I demanded, unwilling to back down.

The raccoon bared his teeth, then took far longer than I would have liked in deciding whether he wanted to talk to me or to bite me.

"Octavius Maxwell Ricardo Edmund Frederick Fulton is his own animal," he said at last, enunciating each word carefully. "He can't be owned by you or anyone else."

Whatever answer I'd expected, it had most definitely not been this. "You kn-n-now him?" I stuttered, dropping to my knees so that I could look the animal in the eye.

He laughed nervously, all his bluster having disappeared in an instant. "Know him? No! I wish I knew him! Even to be standing in his home right now is such a tremendous honor. I can't even begin to—"

"You broke in," I snapped at him in frustration. "There's no honor in that."

The raccoon hung his head and wept. I couldn't tell whether his tears were fake, but this ring-tailed bandit definitely gave both Nan and Octo-Cat a run for their money in the drama department. No matter what I did or where I went, I was always surrounded by thespians.

"Enough blubbering," I blurted out, more than ready to get on with it. "Tell me who you are and why you're here. Are you some kind of weird Octo-Cat fanboy?"

"He prefers his full name, I'll have you know," the raccoon actually had the audacity to correct me. "And I'm not just some random fanboy." He shook his head adamantly, then bared his teeth again in a creepy smile that sent me stumbling backward to put a bit of distance between us. "I'm his biggest fan. Numero uno, baby!"

There weren't many moments in my life when I'd done an actual facepalm. This, however, was one of them. "I didn't know house cats could have fans," I admitted, still in utter disbelief.

The raccoon shot forward and positioned his face mere inches from mine as he cried, "He's not just any house cat, lady! He is the ultimate in animal sophistication."

Okay, it was probably time to move the discussion to finding out whether he had any leads as to where Octo-Cat had gone, but I desperately needed to know how my cat had landed himself such an enthusiastic follower. "Why do you like him so much? How did your, um, fandom get started?"

The raccoon stood higher on his haunches and swept his hand in front of his face theatrically. "It all started one dark and starry night. I was going about my business as usual, spying on some humans, raiding some trash cans, you know, the works. When lo and behold, I found something new and shiny. It caught my eye right away. Not just because it looked valuable, but because the smell... Wow, what an aroma!"

He scooped the empty Fancy Feast can he'd brought in with him up from the floor and held it out to me. "It was the most succulent delicacy I'd ever tasted in all my life, and then to find that each day there was more! Wow, I was the luckiest trash panda in all of Blueberry Bay."

I had to fight hard not to explode with laughter. "Did you just call yourself a tra—you know what? Never mind. Go on."

"Well, naturally, I needed to learn more about from whence this heavenly food had come. So I started to watch. Observe, if you will. And that's when I first saw Octavius. Being the intelligent creature that I am, I realized the food was his and that I was feeding off mere scraps. Made me wonder what other wonderful things he knew about, so I watched some more. Soon I'm learning about Evian and Apple, sun spots, and a million other amazing things. Naturally when I found his collar here, I knew it was the ultimate king piece for my collection. And in I came to see what else I might find or if—for the love of the great raccoon in the sky—I might actually get the chance to meet the great Octavius."

"What's your name?" I asked skeptically. For the first time since Octo-Cat had gone missing, I was actually glad he wasn't around to hear this. I'd always assumed his ego couldn't get any larger... until now.

The raccoon set the empty can of cat food back onto the floor and attempted to place Octo-Cat's collar around his neck. With another off-putting, sharp-toothed smile, he asked, "Would it be too much to ask you to call me Octavius? If I could pick any name that's the one I'd choose. Definitely."

"Yes, definitely way too much." I needed to be firm with this one, else we'd never get anywhere. At least he seemed smart and like he'd remember our conversation after the fact. Perhaps he'd even want to help. "What's your actual name?"

He pouted a lower lip and looked down at his feet. "Pringle."

Okay, that was adorable. So why did he seem embarrassed by it?

"Nice to meet you, Pringle. I'm Angie." I reached out and shook his paw, and the raccoon knew just how to return the friendly gesture. He was definitely smart and definitely familiar with human and cat customs alike.

"So, Pringle. How'd you get a name like that?" I'll be the first to admit this little guy had me enamored—hopeful, too.

"Well, *Angie*," he began with zero hesitation. "It's a long story, but basically when my mother was carrying me and my littermates, Pringles were her number one favorite trash snack. Me being the first born, Pringle became my name. Hey, actually it's not that long of a story, after all. There you have it. The end."

I allowed myself a small laugh before regaining my composure and sharing a bit of information I knew my new friend would not like. "Okay, Pringle. Thanks for the back story, but I've got bad news. Our dear Octavius has gone missing. It's been close to twenty-four hours now, and we have no idea where to find him."

The raccoon lifted both of his tiny black hands to his face and gasped. "Octavius, noooo!" he shouted. "You were far too young and perfect to meet such an untimely end." Pringle then fell backward in a mock faint, and I wondered if he might also be watching a bit of television on the sly when he spied on us during the day.

"Hey. No, none of that!" I cried, nudging him until he sat back up. "Not dead! Why do you jump straight to dead?"

Pringle's eyes widened and began to shine with gaiety. "Then he's alive! Our dear Octavius is alive!"

When I nodded my confirmation, he jumped at least a foot in the air and pumped his fist enthusiastically. What an odd little creature.

"Stop jumping to conclusions and just listen, okay?" A smile snaked across my face when I realized exactly how I could get through to the hyperactive raccoon. "Octavius depends on it. Actually, he depends on you."

"You had me at Octavius," he said, taking a bow, although for the life of me, I didn't know why. "And now you have my rapt attention."

I nodded. "Good. Come meet the rest of the Octavius fan club, and we'll catch you up."

"I'm still the president, because I'm the number one fan," he said, eyeing Charles and Nan with a newfound aggression as we approached.

"Of course you are," I assured him. "You are definitely his biggest fan. I don't think any of us are going to challenge you for that honor."

Pringle smirked as if he'd just won some hugely desirable prize.

Charles waved hello to the newest member of our party. Nan held up her poster board, and I caught the raccoon up on everything we knew so far. Could his passion be the key to cracking this case wide open?

Oh, I sure hoped so.

10

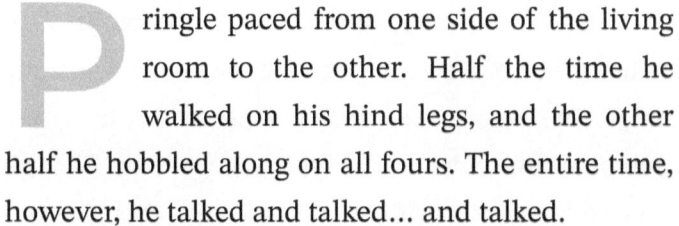

ringle paced from one side of the living room to the other. Half the time he walked on his hind legs, and the other half he hobbled along on all fours. The entire time, however, he talked and talked... and talked.

I barely had time to translate for Nan and Charles before he'd cut me off to continue with his monologue.

"Whoever took Octavius, we're going to make him pay. We're going to make him pay big." The raccoon pounded his tiny black fist into his open palm for emphasis. "I won't rest until he's brought home safely. I won't eat a single—Actually, okay, I'm going to have to eat. A raccoon's gotta keep his strength up if he's going to rescue his cat pal from clear and imminent danger."

"Um, excuse me?" I said, raising my hand to draw Pringle's attention my way. "Have you ever even met Octo-Cat?"

The raccoon sighed and heaved his furry shoulders. "Not yet, but I assume you'll introduce me once he's home again, yeah?" His eyes grew wide, and for a brief moment he stopped pacing and started shaking instead. I assumed it was with excitement.

Although I was tempted to reach out and pet him, I didn't know how he'd take to such an intimate gesture. "I can promise he'd love nothing more than to meet the president of his own personal fan club," I said with a huge grin. "Thank you for being so willing to help us with this."

Pringle stretched on his tiptoes and spread his arms out wide as he boomed, "Of course. This is what I was put on this earth to do. Octavius is a legend, but he's not yet ready to be a memory. He must live another day to inspire animals both near and far." The raccoon pounded his fist on his chest and then kneeled and bowed his head reverently.

Not knowing what to do, I patted him between the ears and said, "Thank you for your service."

He lifted his head but kept his fist held firmly to his chest. "It is an honor to serve him. What is my first assignment?"

Uh-oh. Had I just unwittingly knighted a trash panda?

I blinked hard at the creature who remained kneeling before me. This whole scene would have been hilarious if I weren't so worried about Octo-Cat.

Pringle cleared his throat. "Lady Angela, my assignment?"

"Oh, oh, yes." It took me a second to snap back to reality. So what if the creature before me was half-medieval knight and half-screaming fanboy? He had pledged his service to finding Octo-Cat. We now shared a passion and a cause. Hope sprung anew as I racked my mind for a list of tasks I could give Pringle to keep him busy.

"I need you to talk with the other animals around the forest. Find out if they saw or heard anything that could be useful. After night falls, come back here and keep an eye on things around the house. If you see anything suspicious, be sure to let us know."

"On my honor." Pringle gave me one last

lingering look before racing back out through the cat door and, presumably, setting to work.

"Hopefully he'll be more successful than we were," Charles said, reminding me that I wasn't alone. Sometimes when I got deep into a conversation with an animal, I forgot about the humans nearby.

"If nothing else, at least it will keep him busy," I said with a shrug.

Nan flipped the poster board over and uncapped a purple marker. "Now, dear. I know this won't be easy, but it's time we discussed you a bit more. Or more specifically, who might have it out for you."

A fresh wave of panic bubbled inside me. "Do you think someone kidnapped Octo-Cat to get back at me?"

"Well, it's not like he had any enemies of his own, so I guess it's a possibility." Charles scooted up to me and wrapped an arm around my shoulder. I laid my head on his chest and tried not to feel as if I'd somehow signed my best fur friend's death warrant. When it came right down to it, though, we had no proof he would ever come home again—or that he was even still alive.

"Now, dear. Who hates you most in this world?" Nan asked, completely oblivious to the emotional river that raged within me. She was never one to use a gentle word when a stronger one would do.

Hate, wow. There were people out there who actually hated me. That was, indeed, a tough pill to swallow.

"But also knows you well enough to know that taking your cat would be a huge punishment," Charles added softly.

"Oh, excellent point," Nan said with a giggle. She spied Charles's hand on my shoulder and tossed a wink my way, enjoying this whole mess far too much for my liking.

"Hate's a really strong word," I hedged as I shook free of Charles's arm. Immediately the cold took his place and sent a shiver rushing down my spine.

"It's a strong feeling, too," Nan agreed. "I know it's hard to think about, but I'm almost certain the folks you put in prison aren't too happy with you about that."

I got up and walked across the room, then sank down onto the sofa with a groan. "Okay. First of all, I didn't put them in prison. Their crimes did that. And second, they're *in prison.* How could they have possibly taken Octo-Cat even if they'd wanted to?"

"She's right," Charles told Nan, and they let out

matching sighs. It was eerie how well we all knew each other and had even started to pick up some of each other's mannerisms. "We may be working against a two-man operation here."

"Or a two-woman gig. Girls can be bad, too, you know." She seemed to take perverse pride in this observation. Now that was a really messed-up form of girl power.

"That Peter guy who worked with us briefly certainly didn't like you much," Charles added, referring to Bethany's creepy cousin who had worked as a paralegal at our firm. We'd even been forced to share the same desk. I was definitely happy he'd moved down to Georgia, putting a comfortable number of miles between us.

"Yeah, and didn't another fella get fired after you complained about sexual harassment?" Nan quickly interjected. "Brad, was it?"

"Yes and yes, but both those guys were skeezy," I whined. Was my proud feminist grandmother really giving me a hard time about standing up against inappropriate advances? Unbelievable.

"Brad sexually harassed everyone and should have been fired a long time before I finally complained about him. And by the way, I'm not the only one who complained, either. Meanwhile, Peter seemed to have it out for me from day one. Thank goodness they're both gone now."

Nan frowned and fiddled some with her markers. "I'm not trying to upset you. Just trying to help bring our buddy home."

"Look. I can see we're not really getting anywhere with this line of questioning, so let's back it up," Charles said, jumping graciously to my rescue.

"Yes, and Angie seems quite worked up now, too." Nan came to join me on the couch and placed one aged hand on my knee.

"It's not fun making a list of people who despise you," I told them both. It seemed like this day just kept getting worse and worse. "You should try it and see."

"Oh, nobody dislikes me." Nan fluffed her hair and wiggled in her seat. "I'm just a quirky old grandma."

"Uh-huh." I smirked. At least we'd moved on from compiling our Angie's-worst-enemies list.

Charles came over and sat on my other side. "More and more this looks like it must be tied to Ethel Fulton's estate and somebody who was unhappy about how the inheritance was doled out."

"He's right," Nan said, leaning back into the

hard antique cushion. "The timing is too suspect to be anything else."

"And we're sure he didn't just wander off on his own?" Charles raised one eyebrow and waited.

"No way," Nan and I cried in unison.

He pressed his lips in a thin line and made a *harrumph* sound. "Then that narrows our pool considerably. Since Ethel used our firm for her will, I should be able to get a copy. You'll have to catch me up on all the key players and what we know about them so far, though, since this all happened before I moved to town."

"Should we call Officer Bouchard and let him know?" Nan asked. She'd had a crush on this particular member of local law enforcement for close to a year now. Jeez. Between me and Nan, we were crushing on practically everyone in our small town. Not that either of us ever went out on any dates, but still.

Charles shook his head and frowned. "Let him know what? Unfortunately we haven't got any proof."

"You know what that means, then." Nan pressed down hard on my knee and pushed herself back onto her feet. "We need to go find some."

11

Nan stayed back at the house while Charles and I headed to the law firm so we could grab a copy of Ethel's will along with a list of its beneficiaries.

"There are like thirty people on this," I said with a sigh as I ran through the lengthy legal document a second time. "How do we know which one took Octo-Cat?"

"Let's make a list of addresses and last known contact info," Charles suggested, pulling up a fresh document on his laptop. "Then we can probably eliminate anyone out of state and take things from there."

"I'm going to see what I can learn about our

suspects on social media, too." I fished my phone out of my pocket and waved it between us with a mischievous grin. "People are amazingly transparent when they think nobody is paying attention. Maybe we'll find out who's unhappy about the will or having money problems. Someone's gotta have a clear motive if we dig deep enough."

"I like how your mind works. Have at it," Charles said before turning his full attention toward his computer.

We passed a few hours in this way. I took a page from Nan's book and placed color-coded marks next to each name on the list of beneficiaries, depending on what we learned about that person and how likely it was they might be our catnapper.

"The blue checkmarks are for those people I remember seeing at the will reading," I explained once we'd both completed our research. "Gosh, that feels like it happened forever ago."

My life had changed astronomically since that day. I still remembered coming into the office and getting hounded by Thompson for not having on suitable attire. I borrowed a jacket from my friend Bethany, even though we weren't quite friends yet at that point, then I got electrocuted by the coffee maker, woke up able to speak with Octo-Cat, and—boy—things really escalated from there.

Now I had a talking cat for my best friend, lived in one of the swankiest manor homes in the entire state, and was on the verge of opening up my own private investigation firm.

That is, once I got up the nerve to hand in my resignation notice to Charles.

I swallowed hard and continued walking him through my list of suspects. "The black X means either their profiles are set to private or I couldn't find them. I drew a red circle next to the names of people I thought seemed suspicious or like they could kidnap a cat."

"But almost everyone has a red circle," Charles pointed out with a chuckle that sent a knife straight through me.

"Hey, don't laugh. This is serious." I glowered at him until he quieted down.

"You're right. I'm sorry."

"What did you find?" I asked, hoping desperately that he'd narrowed down the pool a little better than I had.

"Well, only a handful live nearby, so they're probably our most likely suspects." He turned his computer toward me so I could see the list of names and addresses, which appeared to be organized by distance with those closest to us up at the top.

"Great," I said, rising to my feet, ready to go. "Print that out for me, and I'll swing by to check them out now. Wait, actually, I'll just grab a picture real quick."

I picked up my phone and navigated to my camera app, but Charles pushed his laptop lid down with a click.

"No, you won't," he said, keeping his hand firmly on the laptop as he waited for me to back down. Ugh, he was so irritating sometimes. "Whoever took Octo-Cat will definitely recognize you and probably Nan, too."

"So, what?" I demanded, stomping my foot like the overdramatic teenager I once was. "I'm just supposed to do nothing?"

A smile lit up his handsome features, putting me at ease. "I didn't say that. I'll go and check things out myself."

I couldn't help but smile. I loved how he'd taken real ownership in this case, too. "Great, let's go," I said, reaching toward the laptop so I could snag a photo of those addresses.

Charles held up an index finger and wagged it at me. "No, Angie. You're not coming. Trust me with this, okay? I want him back just as much as you do. I'm not going to mess this up. But I do have a court appointment this afternoon, so I'm not going to be able to check out these leads until after work."

I hung my head and tried really hard not to sigh. I knew he was right, but it didn't make the waiting any easier. "Thank you," I murmured at last with great difficulty.

"You're welcome," Charles said. "Now, c'mon, let me take you back home. Maybe Pringle will have discovered something helpful while we were gone."

One could only hope...

* * *

Of course, Pringle hadn't found anything worthwhile in my absence and neither had Nan.

"I wonder what Ethel would have thought of all this hullabaloo if she were still alive to see it," Nan drawled over dinner that evening. She'd busied herself by cooking up a storm in the kitchen, so dinner was a strange yet satisfying combination of dim sum, gnocchi, and empanadas.

"You would never kill me to get to my fortune," Nan asked as she bit into a steamy dumpling and trained a wary eye on me. "Would you?"

I dropped my fork and stared at her, slack-jawed. Luckily, I'd just swallowed a mouthful of pasta, otherwise it would have fallen straight down onto the table. The things my nan said sometimes!

"Kidding," she sang with a merry little titter. "Still, though. Poor Ethel. Betrayed by those she loved most, both in life and in death. She only wanted her beloved feline companion to live out the rest of his days in comfort, but that, too, has created difficulty. The old broad just couldn't win."

She shrugged and took another bite, chewing thoughtfully as we sat in silence. I understood why we were talking about the late Ethel Fulton, but it still made me tremendously sad—especially since in some ways, I was living her life now, or at least in her house. To think, even though Ethel had died with lots of money, it was clear she'd been missing some important things in life.

Like love, family, respect.

Nan said nothing more about it, but the woman I'd seen only at her funeral last year remained solidly at the front of my mind. I owed it to her to make sure her cat maintained his lavish lifestyle, that he was brought home safe and sound. So what if other people didn't exactly understand?

I did, and this was my job. It was also something

I cared deeply about and would fight to put right again.

Octo-Cat was coming home, no matter what it took.

Thankfully, updates from Charles started coming in via text shortly after we'd finished dinner. He messaged after each visit he made to one of Ethel's heirs. At first his messages came relatively close together since he was visiting those who lived in our own Glendale, but eventually they became fewer and farther between.

I lay in bed with my phone beside me, eagerly awaiting each one.

Until I fell asleep.

I dreamt of the early days with Octo-Cat, back when we lived in that tiny rental he hated and were still finding our way around each other. I revisited all my favorite memories—like giving him his very own iPad and eating grilled shrimp together, the day the paperwork came in and I officially adopted him. We'd lived through so many important moments together and had so many more that were yet to come.

We'd caught killers and thieves. We could catch a catnapper, too.

The happy memories quickly gave way to the

scary ones. To high-speed car chases and ominous staircases, visiting a friend in maximum security and staring straight into the eyes of someone who wanted me dead.

A bang sounded from across the room, and I jumped into a sitting position before I'd even had the chance to fully wake up. The image of a shiny pistol flashed behind my eyelids. I'd been threatened by a gun more than once this past year, and—

BANG!

It was coming from the other side of my closed door.

No, it *was* my closed door.

Someone was knocking on it as if their very life depended on me answering and answering fast.

"Nan?" I called as I padded hesitantly over.

"Open up! Open up!" a familiar squeaky voice shouted. "There's been a development."

I flung the door open, and in came Pringle.

He clambered right up onto my bed, blinking hard when I flipped the light switch on. "Ahh, I'm blinded by the light," he said, rubbing at his eyes. "Doesn't that thing have a dimmer?"

"Sorry." I switched off the overhead and turned on my bedside lamp. As I came closer, I noticed that he had a piece of white paper with small colorful blocks pasted on one side.

"Where'd you get that?" I asked, pointing.

"That's what I'm trying to tell you. Someone just slipped this under the front door. I came running, but I wasn't fast enough to see the person's face. Definitely a human, though. Definitely a human. *Here. Take it.*"

My hands shook as I took the paper from Pringle's outstretched paws.

"It's a ransom note," I said in disbelief as I looked over the hasty arrangement of letters that had clearly been cut out from a magazine. "Why go to all this trouble? Why not just type what they wanted to say?"

"Clearly somebody has a flair for the dramatic," Pringle said, baring his teeth and rolling his eyes. "So, what's it say? Huh? Huh?"

I moved the paper closer to the light and read, "You don't belong here. Give up the house, or I kill the cat."

I gasped and dropped the letter as if I'd been burned.

"No way, no way, no way!" Pringle shouted as he jumped on my bed. "Nobody threatens Octavius and gets away with it. What do we do now?"

"I don't know," I answered with a sob. "They didn't give us any directions or tell us a place to send our response."

I'd give them the house if that's what it took, but how? I felt more helpless than ever as I stared into Pringle's dark eyes, praying he had the answer.

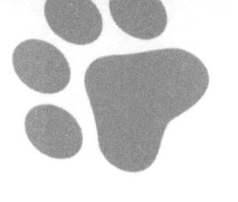

12

"**C**'mon," I told my raccoon accomplice after several moments of tense silence passed between us. "Let's go get you some Fancy Feast."

I took a picture of the ransom note with my phone and forwarded it to both Charles and Nan, then headed for the pantry to prepare a late-night snack for both me and Pringle. I'd already made it about halfway down the stairs when I realized he wasn't following me.

Instead, Pringle stood at the top of the narrow stairway with giant, glistening tears in his dark eyes. "Fancy Feast? For me?" he crooned.

I smiled at the sweet but bizarre forest creature.

"I can also throw in some Evian if that helps to sweeten the deal."

Pringle scampered down the stairs as fast as his four feet could carry him and attached himself to my leg in what I assumed was a grateful hug. "This is the best day of my life," he whispered into my plaid pajama pants. "The very best day."

"Just wait until you meet Octavius," I said with a chuckle, picturing the scene unfold—the look of unadulterated joy on Pringle's face, the likely irritation on my cat's. "I have a feeling he's going to love you," I said anyway. It was true; once Octo-Cat got past the raccoon's enthusiasm, he'd love having someone in his life who appreciated him as much as he appreciated himself.

Pringle stopped in his tracks but quickly started moving again. I absolutely loved how easy it was to make his day. Once I prepared a late-night meal of Fancy Feast and Evian for him—served on disposable dishes rather than Octo-Cat's preferred Lenox set—and grabbed a granola bar for myself, I went to wake Nan with news of the ransom note.

Before I could reach her bedroom, however, my cell phone buzzed in my hand. The call came from a number I didn't recognize, which seemed especially odd this late at night.

Could it be the catnapper calling to talk terms? I'd happily pay whatever he wanted if it meant getting my cat back.

"Hello?" I asked, a quiver of anticipation racing through me.

"Angie, why didn't you call me earlier?" The speaker sounded quite angry, so it took me a moment to place her.

"B-B-Bethany?" I stuttered, finally recognizing my friend's voice. "Where are you?"

"Peter and I made it down to Georgia earlier tonight, and Charles just called to catch me up on everything that happened since we left. First tell me, are you okay?"

"Yeah," I lied for some reason. I'd grown to love Bethany, even though our relationship hadn't always been an easy one. Still, as much as I trusted her, I didn't want her to know how destroyed I was by this latest turn of events. She didn't know my secret, and I planned to keep it that way.

"Do you have any idea who could have wanted to take Octo-Cat?" I asked, my voice shaking.

Bethany didn't hesitate in her response. "Clearly, this has something to do with Ethel's will. Remember how angry everyone was that he got anything at all, let alone that huge trust fund?"

I'd already been thinking along these same lines myself, but there was a part of it that still made absolutely no sense to me. "Yeah, but that was months ago," I added. "Why act on it now?"

She hummed a few beats, then asked, "How long has it been since you moved into Fulton Manor?"

"A couple months," I mumbled as I slipped one of my fingers into my mouth and began to bite at the scraggly fingernail. "Think that has something to do with it? I did get this ransom note that specifically mentions it."

"Of course the house has something to do with it," Bethany exploded after I caught her up. "There's one thing that doesn't quite make sense, though. If the catnapping was supposed to keep you from contesting the arbitration, then why send a ransom note at all? I mean, without Octo-Cat's monthly stipend, you wouldn't be able to afford the house and would have to give it up, anyway. Right?"

I groaned, suddenly feeling like I might pass out. "Thanks for reminding me of just how much is at stake here. But yes, I can't afford my mansion on a part-time paralegal's salary. This isn't House Hunters." My joke fell on deaf ears.

"I'm thinking," Bethany mumbled without giving me even a pity laugh.

"Like thinking you might know who did it?" I chanced. It killed me that I hadn't been able to figure this out yet. Was I missing something big due to my panic? Could my shrewd and logical friend catch something I hadn't been able to?

"Not yet," she answered with a sigh. "But I do know the Fultons a bit better than you do. I may be able to connect some of the dots if I puzzle over this long enough."

"Anything you can do would be very helpful," I said politely. "Thank you, Bethany."

"Hey, I owe you one, anyway." Now she let out a little chuckle. I had no idea what she was talking about, though.

"You do? Why?"

"Um, never mind," she said with another nervous laugh. "Gotta go. Bye!"

Well, that was weird. Bethany was right about one thing, though. The arbitration notice and the ransom note did seem at odds with each other. The note might even establish grounds for delaying the arbitration a bit longer. Could the catnapper mastermind really be so shortsighted?

Charles would know better than me.

I glanced at the tiny digital clock on my phone. It was just past twelve thirty. Since I knew Charles regularly burned the midnight oil, I decided to try giving him a call.

"Hello?" a woman's voice answered coldly.

"Oh, um, Breanne?" I chanced a guess. It gutted me that she had answered his phone at this hour.

"Who else would it be? And why are you calling my boyfriend in the middle of the night. *Hmm?*" Well, apparently, it bothered her just as much that I had reason to call so late at night. Charles was my friend before he was ever her boyfriend, though, and I was willing to bet I knew him better and cared for him more.

"Give me that," I heard Charles say before presumably yanking the phone free of his girl-friend's hands.

"Sorry," I muttered. "I didn't mean to interrupt anything."

Charles sucked air in through his teeth. "You're not interrupting. Breanne just stopped by to say a quick goodnight since we're not going to be able to see each other tomorrow."

Yup, uh-huh. Likely story.

Even though I myself was a twenty-eight-year-old virgin, I knew how the world worked. It made me want to throw up everything in my stomach, but still I understood.

"Charles!" Breanne hissed from the other end of the call. "I haven't got all night to wait around here."

"I've gotta go," my friend said, and he even sounded a little sad about it.

"Bye," I whispered after he'd already disconnected the call.

"Humans are weird," Pringle informed me as he waddled his way over to my side.

"We are," I agreed. "But raccoons are kind of weird, too."

He laughed and used his hands to groom himself following his decadent feast of canned cat food. "You've got that right."

"Do you think he's okay out there?" I asked, not bothering to clarify who I meant.

"Listen, babe. I can't live in a world that doesn't have my boy Octavius in it. You better believe he's okay and that whoever did this is gonna pay—and pay big-time."

I reached over and stroked Pringle's fur. If I closed my eyes, it almost felt like he was my missing friend. Instead of purring, he made a soft chattering noise.

"You know," he said after a while. "I've been thinking that perhaps we should start planning Octavius's welcome home party now. That way we're ready whenever he turns up."

"That's a good idea. Why don't you think it over and then get back to me with what we need?"

"It would be my pleasure." Pringle showed me his toothy, slightly scary smile and then hobbled out through the cat door to begin his preparations.

I clutched the ransom note to my chest and sent up a prayer for Octo-Cat's safe return. There were so many people—and animals—who loved him, who missed him, and needed him home.

13

I couldn't sleep for the rest of that night. Instead, I hung out in the living room with all the lights off as I watched the yard, hoping our mystery ransom note writer might make a second appearance.

I must have nodded off at some point, because the next thing I knew, Nan was pressing a warm mug of coffee into my hands and telling me to "Sit up and catch me up on whatever it is I missed."

"What? Oh." I struggled to straighten myself on the stiff couch, but everything hurt. If the catnapper had made another appearance last night, then I'd surely missed it. Darn me and my biorhythms.

"Someone slipped this under the door," I

informed Nan after finding the letter on the floor near my feet and handing it to her.

She clucked her tongue and shook her head. "Well, someone isn't playing very fair. Are they?"

Suddenly, I couldn't keep it in any longer. I'd tried so hard to be strong, and for what? My stiff upper lip wasn't bringing Octo-Cat home.

And so I cried.

Nan took my coffee mug away and set it on the end table, then wrapped me in a hug and made soft shushing noises.

"Do you think they'd really do what they're threatening?" I sobbed, letting all my worry and anxiety overtake me at last. "That they'd kill Octo-Cat?"

Nan stroked my hair as she spoke. Her words came out soft but determined, true. "In my many years on this earth, I've learned one very important lesson, and I've learned it more than once, I'm afraid."

She sucked in a deep breath, and I pulled away from her embrace so we now sat face-to-face.

"Crazy people will do anything if they think it will help them reach their crazy goals," she said sagely.

This was not the answer I'd wanted to hear.

Nan reached forward and brushed her wrinkled fingers against my cheek, picking up a tear on one of her fingertips. "I've learned another thing, too. People will do anything to save their own hides. And I bet that goes for cats, too. Don't count that cat of ours out yet. He's a survivor."

"Yeah, and he still has four lives left. At least according to him," I added with a sad chuckle, pressing my face against her soft sweater and allowing it to offer some measure of comfort in this painful moment.

"That he does," Nan said as she squeezed me with surprising strength. One day I endeavored to be as fit as my nan. Just maybe not today. "So what's the plan? What do we do next?"

I'd had a lot of time to think about our next steps as I staked out the living room last night. Ultimately, I realized that even if the forest animals didn't know what had happened to Octo-Cat, they might still be our best chance of finding him again. Whoever had taken him probably didn't know I could speak with animals, so they wouldn't be on the lookout for my special crew of furry helpers.

"I know that look," Nan said with a huge, relieved grin. "You already have it all worked out. So go ahead. Catch your dear old nan up."

"I haven't worked everything out yet, but I do have a pretty good idea," I said, twisting my back to try to rid it of the kinks I'd developed last night. "C'mon, I'll tell you all together."

We both slipped on shoes and charged out of the house toward the forest. Nan didn't even question it. Perhaps a part of her already knew what I'd decided.

Maple found us as soon as we reached the tree line. "Hey, it's the peanut butter lady!" she cried from her perch on a low tree branch. "Hi, peanut butter lady!"

I bit my lip and widened my eyes, then exchanged a look with Nan while waiting for Maple to calm down enough to talk to her.

"Hi, Maple," I said with a quick, friendly wave. "My name's Angie by the way. You know, in case you forgot. Have you seen Pringle around this morning?"

Her little squirrel nose twitched and then she hopped onto another nearby tree branch. "Pringle!" she screamed. "The peanut butter lady needs you! Maybe she has more peanut butter to give us."

Maple raced back toward the thick tree trunk and scampered down to the ground at lightning speed. "Do you have more peanut butter?" she asked, pushing both hands down onto my shoe again and again, almost like she was performing CPR on my toes.

"I might," I answered in a sing-song voice. "But first bring me Pringle, please."

"Roger that!" Maple bounded into the woods, leaving me and Nan waiting at the edge of the forest.

"What did that cute critter say?" Nan whispered once Maple was out of view.

I chuckled. Despite her faults, Maple was growing on me as well. If she actually managed to carry out this plan and help us get Octo-Cat back, then I'd make sure I hooked her up with free peanut butter for life. "She wants peanut butter," I explained, "and everything she says pretty much traces back to that one thing."

Nan gasped affectionately. "Oh, then why didn't we bring some with us?"

I shook my head and kept my eyes focused on the trees before us. "Believe me, I've already made that mistake once. As soon as she has her peanut butter, she forgets everything else in the world. I need her to focus long enough to help with our plan. She can have her treat after."

Sure enough, Maple appeared again and zipped past us, running back toward the house. "Be right back!" she cried in an excited squeak.

We watched as Maple approached our front porch and then stopped right in front of it. A big gray fluffball climbed out from underneath and blinked in the sunlight.

"I didn't realize he lived so close to us," Nan said as we both watched the wily squirrel lead the dazed raccoon over to us.

"Neither did I," I grumbled. He must have chewed a hole somewhere to get under there, and I was not happy about the unexpected damage to my already hard-to-maintain house.

"Blessed morning, Lady Angela," Pringle crooned once he and Maple had made their way back to us. So we were still doing the whole medieval thing. Okay.

Even though I preferred reading mysteries and true crime, I'd worked my way through enough fantasy novels to emulate his grandiose speaking patterns.

"And good morrow to you, Sir Pringle." I paused and gave a quick curtsy. Oh, brother. "We come to you today with a most noble quest."

"Why is the peanut butter lady talking all funny?" Maple squeaked but was quickly shushed by the raccoon who was still doing his best to remain in character.

"Yes. Octavius." Pringle confirmed his understanding with a nod.

"It's time we brought him home. Are you and your squire up to the task?" I shifted my gaze toward Maple. As flighty as the little squirrel had proven to be, I was hoping Pringle could do a good job keeping her in line. We'd need both animals to carry out my plan.

"Might I choose my own squire?" Pringle asked with a faltering grin. I couldn't say I blamed him. The raccoon appeared to be of near human intelligence, while the squirrel... well... She sure was cute!

"Goodly Maple will serve you well," I said with a curt nod, then brought one hand up to my mouth and whispered, "Besides, I happen to know she'll do anything for peanut butter."

The squirrel's ears perked up at this, but she remained blessedly quiet.

Pringle bowed his head, whether in defeat or humble acquiescence I couldn't quite say. But he said, "Then reveal your plan to us, and we shall make it so."

Okay, it was show time.

Let's hope my harebrained plan was enough to bring our boy home safe.

14

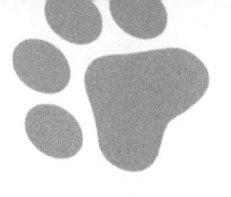
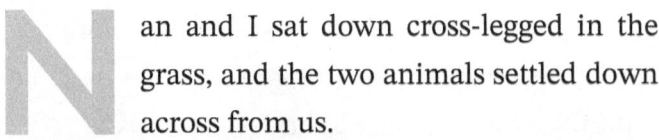

an and I sat down cross-legged in the grass, and the two animals settled down across from us.

"Okay, here's what I'm thinking..." I said, then launched into a winded explanation of my new plan.

"Oh, we should get a pet GPS tracker," Nan added. "I've heard, uh, good things about them." She beamed at me as if I'd just crowned her Ms. Maine. Weird.

"Sure, we can pick one of those up this afternoon," I conceded. It was a good suggestion, but also pretty high tech for a woman who'd only just begun to send and receive text messages.

"Also get some peanut butter while you're out," Maple suggested rather unhelpfully.

"First results, then rewards," Pringle scolded his squirrel squire. Yup, this raccoon was definitely a keeper.

I reached out and gave him a high five, and thanks to his constant human surveillance, Pringle knew just what to do. He may have worshipped Octo-Cat, but he clearly knew more than the idol of his affections.

"That's right," I said, exchanging my goofy grin for a granite jaw and narrowed eyes. "Nothing is more important than bringing Octo-Cat home. Nothing. Not even peanut butter."

Maple gasped.

Pringle cheered.

Nan looked confused but still quite enthusiastic. "What's my role in all this, dear?" she asked, once everyone had quieted again.

This was the tough part. I didn't technically need Nan to carry out my plan, but I knew better than to exclude her.

"You'll keep running command central, and you can help me stay awake tonight, too. Also wardrobe. You're definitely in charge of wardrobe."

She appeared pleased by this. "I'll make cocoa and call the guys."

Ugh, not this again. Why couldn't she have become obsessed with my lack of a love life some other time? It's not as if I were newly single. It had always just been me against the world.

I shook my head emphatically. "The guys? *No.* We don't need Cal and Charles for this."

Nan elbowed me in the ribs. "They're nice distractions, though. Eh?"

I just rolled my eyes rather than dignify her ill-timed matchmaking efforts with a response. "Does everyone understand what they need to do?"

"Yes," Nan and Pringle said in unison. Both looked ready for action.

Maple, however, raised her tiny brown hand. "Um, I forgot," she squeaked meekly.

"It's okay, kid. Come with me and I'll catch you up." Pringle stood on all fours and motioned for the squirrel to follow him back to his under-porch apartment. It looked like we were done playing knights of the round table now—and for that, I was very thankful, indeed.

"I do love a good stakeout," Nan confided in me as we made our way back to the house. "You get the GPS tracker, and I'll head to the supermarket to pick up some snacks and drinks for our little get-together tonight."

I stopped walking and stared at my grand-mother. "Are you really going to invite the guys? This isn't exactly a social event. At least it shouldn't be."

Nan traced her way back to me and wrapped me in a hug. "I know that, dear, but it helps to have good friends by your side when the going gets tough."

Well, I couldn't exactly argue with her there. "Okay," I said, hoping I wouldn't be too embarrassed by whatever she had planned for the evening.

Then again, this was Nan we were dealing with...

Of course I was going to be embarrassed.

* * *

Our stakeout party began at ten that night. Pringle had explained the plan to Maple at least a couple dozen times, and they'd even run test drills both with and without the pet GPS.

Charles and Cal came over right at ten, taking care to hide their vehicles around back. Our entire plan hinged on the ransom note writer coming back that night, and we needed him to assume that the house lay quiet and empty, which meant our party was now taking place in the pitch dark without even a candle to light the room.

We kept our voices low, too, as we whispered and conversed with each other. The whole thing was strangely intimate. We all wore comfortable black sweats—provided by Nan, of course—and sipped warm thermoses of hot cocoa—also provided by Nan.

"Are you sure the person is going to come back tonight?" Cal asked from my left.

"He has to, since he didn't leave any way for Angie to get in touch," Charles answered from my right.

They both sat close enough for me to feel their body heat as it crashed into mine. It didn't escape my notice that these were the two most handsome men I knew now—or had ever known, really. One had brains for days while the other was all brawn. Both had huge hearts, but there in the dark, without their good looks to distract me, I knew there was only one man my heart craved.

And he was the one who was already taken.

Because that's how my life worked. Darn.

"Are you nervous?" Charles whispered in my ear.

"More excited than nervous," I answered, wondering if he felt little zips of electricity jump between us, too.

His phone buzzed in his pocket. We were so close that I felt the vibrations, too. "It's Breanne," he said, pushing a button to send the call straight to voicemail.

A small, petty part inside me did a cartwheel. He was choosing me over her. At least for this. At least for right now.

Around eleven thirty, a sound from outside drew everyone's attention toward the window.

"Shhh," I reminded them all. "We have to hang back, stay out of sight, and trust in the plan now."

"Yes, the plan will set us free," Nan whisper-yelled.

Poor Cal still didn't know I could talk to animals. He thought the plan involved high-tech video cameras and a sophisticated booby trap. Little did he know that one nocturnal raccoon was watching carefully from his spot beneath the porch, and one forgetful but lithe squirrel was already equipped with a GPS and ready to hurl herself into our mysterious catnapper's car the moment the raccoon gave the okay.

Sure enough, a few minutes later, Pringle charged through the cat door to alert us that the plan was underway.

"C'mon, Cal. Why don't you help me in the kitchen?" Nan guided him away before he could set sights on the newly arrived raccoon visitor holding a second ransom note between his paws.

"Good work, Pringle." I grabbed the note and patted him on the head, then Charles and I burst out into the night. We'd already agreed that he would drive, and I'd navigate by following the tiny tracking dot attached to Maple, who had already stowed away in the car and was now being driven to who knew where.

As curious as I was, I didn't even glance at the new ransom note. Instead, I focused on following that blinking dot, hoping it would take us to Octo-Cat and end this whole terrible ordeal once and for all.

Charles drove effortlessly as I called out each turn. We weren't far behind the catnapper now. Soon the three of us would come face-to-face, and I'd be able to demand answers to my many, many questions.

"This is weird," Charles muttered as we pulled into a sleepy suburb. "I know someone who lives here."

"Yeah, well, Glendale is a pretty small town. Most of us do," I said, staring at the phone so that I wouldn't miss a single beat.

"Charles," I shouted in excitement. "The dot stopped!"

This was it. We were getting our boy back, and we were getting him back now.

"Where?" he asked, a darkness I didn't understand overtaking his features.

"Just a few driveways ahead. Looks like it's the—"

"Yellow Cape Cod?" he asked at the same time he pulled into the driveway and transitioned us to park.

"Yeah, how'd you know?" I asked in shock. Was he just a good guesser, or—?

"This is Breanne's house," he revealed with a low growl from deep in his throat.

Uh-oh.

jumped out of the car before Charles even had time to put it fully in park. I caught up with the red-headed realtor on her porch step and yanked on her purse strap until she was finally forced to turn around and face me. "Where's my cat, you...? You... You... *Breanne!*"

"Don't touch me," she snapped back, foisting her designer purse from my grip.

Oh, I wanted to do a whole lot more than touch her. I wasn't really a slapper, but I would have happily ground her expensive, showy purse into the mud. I only held back due to the urgent need to get to my cat. Was he inside? Had Breanne had him this whole time? So many questions.

"Where is he?" I boomed, taking great satisfaction in how rattled my nemesis looked in that moment. If I kept pushing, she'd crack, easy. "Give him to me right now and nobody gets hurt."

She took a step back and pressed herself against the door. "What are you talking about?" she ground out, looking at me as if I'd gone crazy even though all of this was most definitely her fault and not mine.

I took a step closer and got right in her face, so close I could smell her cloying perfume. Gross. "Don't play dumb. I know it's you who's been slipping ransom notes under my door. We followed you here, too. Didn't we, Charles?" I turned back toward my friend, who remained standing by his car, seemingly unable to speak.

"Let me in!" I screamed. "Let me in right now!"

But Breanne stood firm with both arms crossed over her chest. "No. Go away!"

Thankfully, Charles finally snapped out of whatever funk he was in and marched right over, then stepped around us and pushed the door open.

"How could you?" he asked his horrible, no-good girlfriend, but I didn't stick around to hear her answer.

Once inside, I began to shout for my cat at the top of my lungs. But even after tearing through the entire house, I still couldn't find him. "Octo-Cat! Octo-Cat! Are you here? Come out! It's safe!"

When no answer came, I rounded on Breanne once more. "Where is he? Why did you take him? How could you?"

"I don't have your stupid cat, and I don't owe you anything," she answered with a sniff and looked away, almost as if she might feel a little guilty. Yeah, right. I was most definitely not buying that.

"I think you owe me some answers, though," Charles interjected. "Did you really steal Angie's cat and send her threatening letters? Why would you do that?"

"You both need to calm down," she muttered through clenched teeth. "I don't have the cat. Okay?"

"Sorry. I'm not buying it. You delivered the letters. We caught you in the act," I exploded.

Breanne narrowed her gaze, looking past Charles so she could focus all of her venom and hostility right on me. "Fine. I'll admit it. That was me. But I'm not the one who wrote them."

"Who did? Stop stalling, and tell me what you know," I demanded. Why wouldn't she just come out with it already? It's not like either of us treasured spending time together, and this was serious.

Breanne shook her head. "I don't know." She took a step back when Charles stepped back so that we now stood side-by-side. Now we were united against her, and that seemed to break her. Apparently, she'd expected him to take her side in all this.

"How could you not know?" I couldn't see Charles's face as he spoke, but his disappointment came out loud and clear. "Why would you ever agree to be a part of this? And then to not get all the answers?" He cleared his throat before continuing. "I thought you were smarter than that, Bree. Kinder, too."

"I didn't," I spat.

Breanne had never liked me, and I'd never liked her. I wasn't surprised she'd want to hurt me, but it did startle me that she was involved in this terrible thing. Breanne had absolutely no link to Ethel Fulton's estate, so why would she even get involved in the first place?

"It's not a big deal," Bree cried. "So, seriously, calm down. You know my income has been down ever since my brother was branded a murderer. So when an anonymous client turned up and promised me a big commission in my future plus a generous cash infusion now, how could I say no? It's not like I'm hurting anyone. We were just trying to spook you out of that house of yours."

"You threatened to kill my cat!" I shook with rage now that I had someone to blame but still had zero idea where my cat might be.

"No, I didn't do that. I didn't write the letters. And seriously, who would kill a cat? That's taking things a little too far." She seemed to be losing steam by the minute but still wouldn't admit she'd done a single thing wrong.

"But extortion is just fine," Charles grumbled as he narrowed his eyes at Breanne. "Really, Bree. I thought I knew you."

"You do know me, which is why I thought you'd understand," she pleaded. "You know how hard things have been lately."

"But you're working through that," he argued. "Honest work. Not blackmail and threats." Despite my anger, it struck me as a bit funny that Charles was berating his girlfriend for blackmailing me when he'd done the same thing to get my help on a difficult case. Granted, he never would have actually hurt me. Breanne, on the other hand…

"No," she insisted. "I'm trying to, but not succeeding. And you know why? Everyone thinks my brother's this monster, even after he was acquitted, and it's all her fault." She raised a shaky finger toward me. If looks could kill...

Charles put his hand on my shoulder. "She helped me get him acquitted. How have you conveniently forgotten that little part of the story?"

Breanne shrugged. "Her mother, though. That news anchor woman. She's the one who convinced all of Blueberry Bay that Brock was guilty, and even after he was proven innocent, they've had a hard time changing their minds. Oh, and don't think I've missed the fact that you're trying to steal my boyfriend right out from under my nose."

"Jeez, what is wrong with you?" Charles yelled. "Angie and I are just friends. And that doesn't even really matter anyway, because you and I are officially through."

"Charles, baby. Don't be like that," Bree begged, approaching him with hands raised in supplication.

He turned from her and strode toward the front door. "I'll wait for you in the car," he informed me before disappearing outside.

"Do you really not know who was sending the letters?" I asked gently. As much as I hated Breanne, she had just been dumped and seemed pretty upset by it. Besides, yelling at her wasn't getting any of the answers I needed, but maybe a bit of kindness would.

"I really don't know," she said with a sniff. "Now please... Just... Just go away."

I studied her for a moment before finally turning away and following Charles outside. I found him behind the wheel of his car with this head down and tears spilling down both cheeks. "Are you okay?"

He sat up straighter and cleared his throat. "I should have known better. I've been so stupid."

"I'm sorry," I said, because it seemed like the best response given the situation. "Do you want to talk about it?"

"Honestly," he said, pulling the car back out of the driveway. "I kind of want to forget it ever happened. I can't believe I wasted so many months of my life on her."

I found myself torn between wanting to be a good friend to Charles and wanting to scream *I told you so* from the top of my lungs. I'd always known Breanne was a bad egg, but I'd never known just how rotten she'd become, never would have suspected she'd go to such drastic lengths to make my life miserable.

"I'm so sorry she did this to you," he said,

keeping his eyes glued firmly to the road ahead. "I wanted to find Octo-Cat before, but now it feels like it's my duty, like somehow this is partially my fault. I know I'm a big part of the reason she hates you, and it's up to me to make things right."

"Charles, none of this is your fault."

"It feels that way, though."

I put a conciliatory hand on his forearm. "I accept your help, but not because you owe me anything. Thank you for being such a good friend."

We drove back to my house in utter silence. Had Charles meant it when he told Breanne we were only friends? Or had he also been harboring a secret crush on me all these months?

I pushed these questions from my already over-cluttered brain. Only one question mattered now, and it needed all our focus...

Where was Octo-Cat?

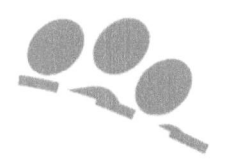

16

Back at my house, Nan and Cal were waiting for Charles's and my return with every light on the main floor at full blast.

Cal popped to his feet when we entered. "Did you find him?"

"No," I said, accepting a fresh mug of cocoa from Nan, who was clearly enjoying her role as stakeout hostess.

"Did you find who was leaving the notes?" she asked with large eyes.

"Yeah, we did." I bit my lip, not wanting to be the one to break this news to Breanne's twin brother, especially since she'd used his unfairly earned bad reputation as an excuse for getting involved in her shady dealings.

"It was Breanne," Charles answered for me. His voice brooked no arguments. I'd never seen him so livid about anything in all the months I'd known him.

"You mean, your girlfriend?" Nan looked from one man to the other and frowned. "And your sister?"

"She's my ex now," Charles said with a sigh.

Nan didn't even try to hide her happiness at this news. She even wrapped an arm around me and squeezed me to her side. "Good. She wasn't right for you anyway."

I about died when she shot me what she must have assumed was a surreptitious wink.

Charles saw it plain as day, but at least it made him smile.

Cal, however, seemed to be the most upset of everyone. "Why would she do something like that?" He sank down onto the couch and dragged both hands through his hair. "Oh, wait. It's because of me. Isn't it?"

"It's not your fault you got framed for murder," I pointed out gently.

"It sure feels like it, though."

"Charles is blaming himself, too," I said. "But, believe me, this is nobody's fault except Breanne's."

"Okay," Nan shouted, drawing everyone's attention to her. "Enough with the pity party. We have work to do."

"What work? We reached a dead end with Breanne. She says she doesn't know who was paying her to drop off the letters." Charles paced around the living room like a caged lion ready to pounce.

"I'm going to go talk to her." Cal rose to his feet and marched toward the front door. "Call me if you need me."

The door slammed shut, and we all took a collective breath in.

"Charles, look at me." Nan walked right up to him and stood on her tiptoes in an effort to bring her face closer to his.

He stopped pacing, the pent-up energy visible in the bulging veins that had risen to the surface of his neck and forearms. This was killing him.

"I know you're feeling down in the dumps right about now, but you and that woman were never right for each other anyway," Nan said firmly. "So, stop mulligrubbing, and fire up that big, beautiful brain of yours again. We're going to need it to bring our kitty boy home safely."

"Maybe we didn't get anywhere with Bree," I told Charles much gentler than Nan had just spoken to him. "But that doesn't mean we're at a dead end, either. We still have the list of beneficiaries from Ethel's will, and you only checked out the local ones, right?"

He nodded but said nothing. I briefly wondered whether he was holding back tears or shouts. Maybe both.

After grabbing his hand in mine, I gave it a reassuring squeeze. "Then I say it's time we take a little road trip. If someone needed to pay Breanne to drop off those letters, chances are they don't live close enough to do it themselves."

"I'll stay here with the animals in case anything else goes down at mission central," Nan volunteered.

"Charles?" I asked. "I know you're having a really hard time with all of this right now, but I could really use a friend by my side. Are you in?"

He dropped his gaze toward the floor and nodded as if a hundred-pound weight was pushing down on his neck. "I'm in," he groaned.

I wrapped my arms around Charles and gave

him a tight hug. "Thank you," I murmured. "But first before we go, we need to make a quick stop off at the twenty-four-hour market and swing back by Bree's real quick, too."

He studied me in horror. It seemed our opinions about Breanne finally matched, although I hated the circumstances. Unfortunately, we didn't have much of a choice as to whether or not to return to her house that night.

"I'm pretty sure we forgot Maple there," I admitted with a flippant shrug, even though I was beating myself up about having left a man—*er*, a squirrel—behind on our mission. "I figure we should come prepared with an apology and peanut butter, thus our other stop. C'mon, let's go."

Given that our stakeout party had started at ten that night, neither Charles nor I had slept recently. Still, I doubted either of us could have grabbed even a few winks if we'd tried—not with all that was weighing on our minds. Instead, we grabbed a case of the cold espresso drinks—the ones Nan always said tasted like chalk—from my fridge and set off on our next great fact-finding adventure.

"Who should we pay a visit to first?" Charles asked once we'd made it to the main road that ran through our tiny town of Glendale.

"Ethel's niece, Anne," I said definitively, pointing to her name on the printout Charles had given me. "She gave off definite creepy vibes when last we met."

"Creepy as in catnapper creepy?" Charles asked with a lopsided grin. He adjusted his hands on the wheel and settled back in his seat. Now that we'd rescued Maple from Breanne's house and moved past that portion of our night, he seemed to be returning to his normal relaxed self.

"Creepy as in she was on my short list of murder suspects creepy." I then filled him in on my various run-ins with the eerie older woman.

"Definitely creepy," Charles agreed. "So she really broke into Ethel's house?"

"Yup, but seeing as I'd also broken in, I decided to let that one pass." I began to fiddle with a hangnail absentmindedly. Even though Charles and I were back to our usual easy banter, something important had changed. Now I was wondering what every glance, touch, and word meant, whether it might imply that he felt how I did.

I pinched the skin on my wrist to force myself to

focus on finding Octo-Cat rather than finding out what Charles may or may not feel for me.

Luckily, he had to keep his focus on driving, which meant he missed all the weirdness I was serving up in the passenger seat beside him. "But you said she was there to scout out antiques and other valuables she wanted to keep for herself, right?"

"Yeah, and if Octo-Cat and I hadn't showed up to stop her, I'm pretty sure she would have taken it all."

"That's what she said." Charles suppressed a boyish chuckle, and I gave him a playful slap over the center console.

"C'mon. We're both grown-ups here."

Charles broke out laughing again.

"I'm going to let that go, since it's already been a long night and we're just getting started," I said graciously. "Anyway, yeah, my gut says it's Anne. Nobody else really left much of an impression, to be honest."

"Well, then I guess we're headed into Boston. At least we'll beat the morning rush."

We both surveyed the darkness ahead as I plugged Anne's address into the GPS on my phone. "It's almost a four-hour drive," I whined.

"It could have been worse," Charles said with a shrug. "Ethel had family as far away as Oregon. Now there's a drive."

"What do we do if it's not Anne?" I wondered aloud. "Where do we go next?"

He reached for my hand and held it in his. "We're not going to think like that. Just focus on finding Octo-Cat and bringing him home. The in-between details aren't important. And if your gut is saying Anne did it, then that's what I believe, too." He raised my hand to his lips and gave my knuckles a quick kiss before letting go.

Despite the fact that this small gesture of kindness sent my heart cartwheeling and my stomach loop-de-looping, the feel of his lips on my skin did more than any anti-anxiety pill ever could. Charles believed in this, believed we could do it.

And now so did I.

17

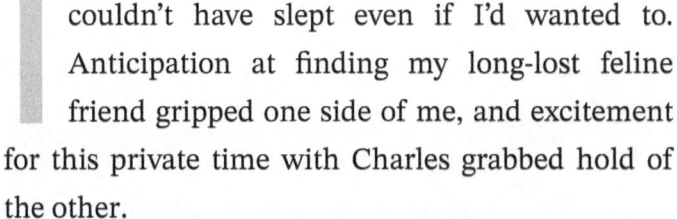

couldn't have slept even if I'd wanted to. Anticipation at finding my long-lost feline friend gripped one side of me, and excitement for this private time with Charles grabbed hold of the other.

For so long I'd wished that he would just break up with Breanne already, and now he had. Might he also see that it had always been the two of us who were meant for each other? I'd tried to put my feelings for Charles aside for months now, but nothing ever worked.

He'd defended Cal against that double murder charge with everything he had. He accepted my ability to speak with animals and never made me feel weird because of it. He'd taken in two homeless, traumatized cats after they'd accidentally killed their owner. He'd just always been there, always been good and kind.

"What are you thinking about?" he asked me now.

I yawned to buy myself some time. "Just sleepy."

"You better not fall asleep on me," he teased. "Your shift is coming up soon."

"Pull over. I'll take it now." Driving would be a nice distraction from all the thoughts fighting to take center stage in my mind.

Charles glanced toward me, then back to the road. "You sure about that?"

"I'm awake, I promise. But if it makes you feel better, I'll shotgun another one of these coffee things." I picked up one of the small blue and brown cans and gave it a good shake.

"Okay, but after that you're cut off." He turned up the music and shuffled through a few songs before landing on one of my favorite '80s hair metal jams.

"It's a myth, you know," I said while bobbing my head along to the heavy, soul-filling beat.

Charles stopped singing along with the track and risked a quick glance my way. "What is?"

I shrugged. "That too much caffeine will either stop your heart or make it explode." As it was, my heart was still beating wildly like a caged animal rattling against its bars. No amount of coffee would change that, either.

It was all Charles, my dream guy. Heaven help me.

When the song ended, Charles put away his air keytar and pulled onto the side of the road so we could switch seats.

"Are you sad?" I asked him when a slow jam took over the speakers and he had to put away his air keytar for a second time. "About Breanne?"

"Angry, more like." He flipped through his playlist again, and this time chose something hard, angsty, and most definitely not from my favorite musical era.

"Do you think you'll forgive her? That the two of you will get back together?" I yelled over the shouty, migraine-inducing music.

He took the hint and lowered the volume. His eyes stayed firmly fixed to my profile as he asked, "Do you think we should?"

I felt a flush rise to my cheeks and hoped he didn't notice. "No," I answered honestly.

"Yeah. Neither do I," he said, crossing his arms

and leaning his face against the cold glass of the window with a sigh. "We were never really right for each other anyway."

"Then why'd you stay together so long?"

Yeah, I was most definitely being nosy, but I also needed to know where things stood, and Charles seemed more than willing to share. Plus we had a lot of time left to kill before we reached Anne's Boston-based bungalow.

"That's a good question," he answered after a short pause.

When I glanced over toward him, his eyes were closed, and he wore a subtle smile on his face. "You don't have to answer, if you don't want," I offered, hoping like heck he wouldn't accept.

He sighed and shifted in his seat, his brow furrowed in a pained look. "I think I was just lonely after having moved so far away to start my new life in Blueberry Bay. I was trying to put down roots."

"Like with the house and the cats," I suggested. *See, there are other ways to build a life. No Breanne Calhoun required.*

"Yeah, and the firm. I never thought I'd make senior partner so fast or that we'd have so much turnover with our associates. It's kept me very busy.

Perhaps too busy to really pay attention to what was going on with me and Breanne."

Well, this was a fresh, new perspective. "What do you mean?"

"I guess that it was just easier to keep dating her, to maintain status quo, you know?"

"No," I answered honestly. "I really don't."

He took a deep breath and squinted over at me for a moment before pressing his eyelids shut once more. "I always liked spending time with Breanne. I know she hated you, but she was always nice to me. I enjoyed being with her, and that was the crucial part. I enjoyed it. It was nice. Fine. Not something I craved. I never counted down the hours until I could see her again. I never let it distract me from work or anything else I had going on in my life. She filled a hole in my life, but didn't overfill it, I guess."

"That's what she said," I muttered when I sensed the mood was getting too serious.

Charles chuckled softly but stayed on topic anyway. "Maybe I was unfair to her, letting it go on as long as it did. I'd feel guilty if I weren't so furious about what she did to you."

"Don't worry about me," I said. "I'll be just fine."

"I know you will be. You're the strongest person

I know," he said softly as another rush of heat flooded my cheeks.

Was now the time I should confess how I felt about him?

It seemed he had just offered me the perfect segue, and this was the first time in our relationship I actually could share my feelings without it getting in the way of a shared case at work or having an angry girlfriend to answer to. We were both free to explore what had been there between us from the very start.

Now was as good a time as there had ever been. I needed to be brave. This was it...

"Charles..." I mumbled, glancing over toward him. There was so much that needed to be said.

But now wasn't the time, seeing as Charles was fast asleep.

I'd never been great at city driving, but luckily we reached Boston before the sun even had its chance to rise for the day. I woke Charles right around the time the GPS informed me we had five minutes left in our drive.

"Why'd you let me sleep so long?" he exclaimed with a groan.

"It seemed like you needed it," I said with a smile. I'd been so close to revealing everything, all my secret longings and wishes. Thank goodness he had nodded off and saved me—saved both of us—from myself. I needed to focus on Octo-Cat right now. We both did.

Charles straightened in his seat and slapped his cheeks a few times to wake himself a bit more. "So, what's the plan?"

Luckily, I'd had a lot of time to think things over as I drove with only Charles's eclectic playlist to keep me company on the long, lonely road. "I thought you could be the one to approach her. Make some excuse about the estate and the arbitration. Use a lot of legal terms, and I'm sure she won't question you."

He nodded, then rubbed the sleep from his eyes. "Okay. Then what?"

"Get her to invite you inside. Excuse yourself to use the bathroom. Then see if you can find him."

"That's a good plan, but..." He sighed and stretched his legs out in front of him, then turned back toward me. "Don't you think it will be suspicious that we're doing all this before six a.m.?"

"Yeah, probably," I admitted. It looked like we'd just fallen into a hurry up and wait trap. I hated those.

Charles seemed unbothered by the inconvenient hour. He smiled over at me and asked, "Don't you think it would be better if we grabbed some breakfast first and then came back at a more reasonable hour so we can sell our story better?"

"Yeah, probably," I agreed.

His smile widened, and he pointed at a big, bright diner sign just down the road. "Then, c'mon. Let's load up on eggs and bacon. My treat."

I nodded and turned into the parking lot, wishing we would have timed this a little better but happy we were at least making some form of progress.

Charles held open the door for me, which was a small thing but felt monumentally huge. "Ladies first," he said.

And I blushed.

Me and my stupid crush.

18

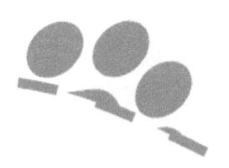

Breakfast was slow, leisurely, and full of unspoken angst on my part. At around seven thirty, Charles handed the waitress his credit card and asked if I was ready to head over to Anne's place.

Oh, was I ever.

"Thanks for the hot meal," I mumbled shyly. "I needed that."

He looped an arm over my shoulders as we made our way through the mostly empty diner. "No thanks needed between friends."

Friends, right.

"How do you think Octo-Cat will react once we find him?" I asked, once again trying to pull my head back into the game we were actually playing here.

Charles smiled and widened his eyes. "My money's on one very grateful kitty. There may even be licks and scritches involved."

I giggled as he held the door open for me on the way out. "I'll take that bet, because I'm pretty sure he's going to demand a proper meal and then chastise us for taking so long to find him."

"Oh, c'mon," Charles said, joining me in my laughter. "Of course he's going to be grateful. Why would he complain after all we've been through?"

"First agree to the bet," I insisted, not making eye contact with him as we crossed the parking lot. "Twenty bucks?"

"You're on." Charles slid behind the steering wheel, and I climbed into the passenger seat. "Now explain yourself, Russo."

"Let's just say that I'm the only one who can actually understand him, and well... I might just censor out his catittude when translating for you and Nan." I just couldn't stop smiling. I missed Octo-Cat and his grandiose way of doing absolutely everything.

"Wait!" Charles shifted in his seat and faced me

head-on. "Has he been saying awful things about me all this time? And here I had no idea."

I laughed again. It felt so good to laugh. Almost like Octo-Cat was here with us now. "Not lots of bad things. He does call you UpChuck, though."

"What a bratty cat!" Charles cried. "First, let's get him home safe and sound, and then I'm going to come up with an equally disgusting nickname for him."

"You've got it," I said between laughs.

Oh, I couldn't wait to see how this played out.

We reached Anne's bungalow about five minutes later. We were early, but some of the neighbor kids were already milling around at what appeared to be the local bus stop.

"I'll wait here. You go ahead." I gave Charles a little push, then watched as he marched confidently up to Anne's front door, briefcase in hand. Despite the five o'clock shadow and noticeable bags under his eyes, he certainly looked the part of a lawyer visiting on official estate business.

Let's just hope Anne would buy it.

He pressed the doorbell and waited.

When nothing happened, he pressed again.

"Maybe it's broken," I texted rather than calling

out, just in case Anne remembered me and chose to hide for that reason alone. "Try knocking."

Charles knocked several times, but nobody came. If Anne was inside, she clearly refused to answer the door.

I scrambled out of the car and joined Charles on the porch. "Open up, Anne Fulton!" I shouted into the hard wood of the door. "We know you're in there!"

"Um, excuse me," a woman's voice called from the next condo over. "Are you looking for Anne?"

Well, it looked like I wasn't the only one with ace detective skills around here. Charles and I both backed down off the porch and came to join the woman where her yard met up with Anne's.

"Yes," he said with a nod in greeting. "We're from the firm representing her late aunt's estate and have some very important developments to discuss."

The woman frowned and shook her head. "I'm so sorry. You just missed her. Well, missed her by a few days actually. She's on vacation this week. I've been collecting her mail and watering her flowerbeds. Can I take a message for you?"

"Thank you, but that's all right," I said, forcing a smile. It wasn't the neighbor's fault that Anne was nowhere to be found. It was, however, her fault that we couldn't break in to explore the premises.

"Do you know what day she left?" Charles asked intelligently.

"Tuesday morning, bright and early."

"Great, thanks. You've been a huge help," he said with another nod to say goodbye.

I followed him back to the car. Neither of us spoke until the neighbor woman gave us one final wave and walked back into her condo.

"The timelines match up perfectly," he said, his hands shaking with excitement. "Anne left Boston early enough to take Octo-Cat. For all we know, she's had him this whole time."

"Do you think she's hanging out somewhere in Blueberry Bay?"

"Call Nan. She'll know what to do on her end. We can discuss the rest on our way back home."

Sure enough, Nan picked up on the first ring, then immediately launched into her plan of attack once I'd caught her up on what had gone down in Boston. "If that wretched woman's staying anywhere near here, I'll find her. I have the perfect costume for this role."

"What role?" I asked.

"Why, of the forgetful but well-intentioned elderly aunt, of course. Nobody ever suspects the little old lady, you know. They'll hand over her room number in a heartbeat, and when I find her, I'll—"

"You'll wait for me and Charles," I interrupted. "Promise me, you'll wait for us."

"Fine. I'll find her and then I'll stake things out until the B team can arrive."

"So we're the B team now?" I asked with a chuckle.

"We can't all be the A team, dear. Now get that man to drive fast, so we can bust in on the bad gal and take back what's ours."

After hanging up with Nan, I turned to Charles with a giant grin and asked, "How fast are you willing to book it back there?"

He pressed down a bit harder on the accelerator, and we were off.

I felt confident we'd find Octo-Cat before the day was through, but I still had questions. Mainly, if Anne was staying locally, why would she have hired

Breanne to hand-deliver her ransom notes? And also, why do all this now when the arbitration for Ethel's estate was already scheduled for tomorrow?

Charles didn't have any good answers, either, which meant the best we could hope for was a crazed confession when we caught Anne red-handed later that morning—or afternoon, depending on the traffic we had to fight coming back home.

We were still a couple hours outside of Glendale when Nan called. I put the phone on speaker so Charles could hear, too.

"The eagle is in the nest!" she shouted into the phone. "I repeat, the eagle is in the nest!"

"Does this mean you found Anne?" I asked, hope rising in me like a shiny, Mylar balloon floating toward the ceiling.

Nan giggled. "Of course we found her. We are the A Team, after all."

I let out a giant, relieved sigh. We were so close to bringing our boy home. Something about what Nan had said didn't quite make sense, though, so I asked, "Awesome, so I just have two questions. Where are you, and who else is part of that "we" you just mentioned?"

"Um, just a second, dear." Nan's track pants

swished, and a moment later she explained, "Sorry, I wanted to get a bit of privacy for this part. I'm with Cal and his sister."

"You're with Breanne?" I growled, immediately tensing up all over again. "Why?"

"Relax. I know we hate her, but she's the one who found out where Anne was staying and led us straight to her."

Charles sent me a panicked glance, and I made a gun out of my thumb and index finger and pointed it at my head with a grimace.

"Are you ready for the address?" Nan asked. Apparently, we were done talking about both Breanne and Anne now.

I agreed. No more talking. It was time for action.

I jotted the address down and made Nan promise to text it over, too. Apparently, Anne had taken a motel room in the nearby town of Cooper Cove. And we'd be there in less than two hours.

"You got that twenty bucks ready?" I asked Charles. Soon I'd be collecting on our little bet, but even more importantly, soon I'd have my cat back and would finally be able to figure out why he was taken in the first place.

This was it. Everything was about to go down.

Anne didn't stand a chance.

I was one angry cat-mama, and I was coming for her.

19

Charles and I made it to that dingy motel in Cooper Cove in record time. When we arrived, we found Nan waiting with the Calhoun twins in the parking lot. Nan and Charles sat together in Nan's sports coupe while Breanne sat parked a few spots away, flipping through a giant stack of papers in the driver's seat of her luxury SUV.

The moment Charles and I pulled into that parking lot, everyone scrambled out of their cars and rushed over to join us.

Cal gave me a huge hug. "Welcome back," he said with a charming grin.

Breanne tried to hug Charles, but he was having none of that.

"Let's do this!" Nan let out a battle cry and led the charge up the outdoor staircase and toward motel room number twenty-six.

The rest of us followed like obedient little ducklings.

We found the room, third on the right, after exiting the narrow stairway. Charles nudged his way to the front of our pack and banged on the door. "Open up," he called, his voice much deeper than usual. Maybe to sound more intimidating. Yeah, because that was the way to get her to voluntarily open the door.

"Are you sure Anne's even in there?" I asked. A frustrating sense of déjà vu had already begun to set in. What if this was Boston all over again?

"Anne? No," Nan admitted with a look of determination that didn't waver. "The catnapper? Yes."

"How...?" I began. My voice shook just as much as my hands in that moment.

Cal generously explained the situation to Charles and me, who were now both utterly confused. "So hang on a sec. Here's what happened. First off, Breanne felt really bad about her role in all of this, so she agreed to help."

"It's true. I did. *I do.*" Bree placed a hand on Charles's arm, but he ripped it away.

"I'd prefer to hear this from your brother, thank you very much," he grumbled, refusing to even look at his recent ex.

Cal waited until I nodded for him to go ahead. "Well, um, Bree sent an email since that was the only form of contact she had for the ransom note writer, and basically, well, she said that the plan had worked and that you had agreed to give up the house, Angie." The poor guy seemed so nervous. It was obvious he didn't like being the middleman in this lovers' spat, and I couldn't say I blamed him.

When Cal hesitated again, Breanne took over the recap. "I told the person that I had the preliminary paperwork and that we needed to meet face-to-face in order to move on with the next phase of the plan. About an hour later, I was sent this address and room number."

"Have you been inside yet?" I asked, glancing back toward the closed door.

"No, we were waiting for you," Nan said. "We wouldn't have solved the case without you."

"Yes, unfortunately, we've been here for quite a while now," Bree snapped, focusing all her hostility on me now that Charles had made it clear he didn't want to have anything to do with her. "So can we please just get this over with already? I have other things to do today, you know."

"Like delivering more ransom notes?" Nan quipped, laughing at her own joke.

It may not have been the most mature decision, but I couldn't resist giving her a high five for that perfect joke.

Bree scowled at both of us, reminding me how serious this situation was.

"She's not answering," I muttered, staring at the cheap motel door and wishing I had the power to see right through it. "Why is she not answering?"

Nan cleared her throat and held up one pointer finger. "Housekeeping," she called out happily, giving the door an upbeat series of knocks.

The door in front of us remained closed, but the one to the next room opened a crack and a middle-aged man peeked his head out. "Housekeeping?" he asked us with a confused expression.

"They just went inside another room. Looks like you've got a bit of time to make yourself decent," Nan said with a flirtatious wink.

"Wait," I cried just as the door was closing the last bit of the way.

The man nudged it open a few inches and stared at me curiously.

"Did you happen to run into the woman who was staying in this room? We were supposed to get together today, but she's not answering."

He shook his head. "Sorry, no. I just got in last night."

Click. The door closed again.

"Oh, this is ridiculous," Breanne groused. "C'mon," she told Cal, grabbing his arm and pulling him along. "We'll go check with the front desk. You can all stay here."

Nan, Charles, and I waited in silence. What was left to say? Octo-Cat might be in the room, but he might also not be. It was like Schrödinger's cat but without the box and hopefully without the dead cat, too.

Thankfully, it only took five minutes for the twins to return.

"The occupant checked out," Cal explained with a sad shake of his head. "And we were so close, too. I'm sorry, Angie."

Nan patted Cal on the bicep. "That's okay, dear. Did they give us a name?"

"No, they wouldn't," Bree seethed. "Some ridiculous code of privacy or something."

Angry tears burned at my eyes and throat. "Now what?" I screamed at the closed door.

Charles and Nan hugged me from either side, which apparently was enough to send Bree tip-tapping out of there on her impossibly high heels. "It's been swell," she said, waving as she walked away. "Keep me posted. Or, you know, don't. Whatever."

"What a piece of work, that one. You know I never did much care for her," a smooth, haughty voice informed us from below.

"Not now, Octo-Cat," I murmured. "We have to figure out what we're going to do next."

Wait... Was that...? *Oh!*

My head snapped up, and I ran to the edge of the outdoor hallway so fast I practically tumbled straight over the edge.

"Watch it there," Charles cried, looping his arms around my waist and catching me just in time.

But I didn't care about the fact my crush held me tight or that I'd almost fallen a full story. All I cared about was the blurry, brown-and-black-striped figure that sat in the small courtyard below, regarding me irritably.

"You know..." Octo-Cat said slowly, his way of making sure I understood. "I've been gone for three whole days. That's three whole days drinking tap water and choking down store brand cat food. *Three days* without my iPad or cat door. Do you know how much I've suffered? Honestly, Angela, what took you so long?"

I choked on a sob and jabbed Charles with my elbow. "Give me twenty bucks," I said, holding out my hand.

"Are you going to take me home now?" Octo-Cat demanded. "I'm not stepping a paw on that dirty cement again, and I've had more than enough of an adventure for this week, thank you very much."

I wiped my nose on the back of my arm and ran down the stairs. When I reached Octo-Cat, I scooped him up into my arms and squeezed him to my chest.

"Gross!" he protested. "I just finished my mid-day ministrations, and now you've gone and wiped your germs all on me. Unhand me, you filthy human. Unhand me right now."

I set him back on the grass and laughed like a crazy person. I didn't care what anyone thought. This was one of the very best days of my entire life. Octo-Cat was here, and he was no worse for the wear—no matter what *he* claimed. I did wonder, though...

I stared into his glinting amber eyes as I asked,

"How are you here on your own? Where's the person who took you?"

My tabby jumped up onto a nearby bench seat and waved his paw around dramatically. Whatever he was about to say, it was sure to be entertaining and to overexaggerate his importance. Ahh, it was so good to have him back.

Octo-Cat smiled as he launched into his harrowing tale. "Well, she was leaving in a hurry a couple hours back. She tried to take me with her, but I let these babies out, and—"

Schwink. His claws popped out in all their menacing glory.

"Let's just say I won that particular fight." He laughed in that favorite villainous way of his.

"You said *she.* Do you know who took you? Was it a woman?"

He shrugged his adorable little kitty shoulders. "It was definitely a person I've seen before. I'm pretty sure it was one of Ethel's relatives, and I am at least sixty percent sure the person was a female."

I patted him between his ears. "Good work." He still had a hard time telling humans apart, but he was getting better. Slowly but surely, he was getting better, and he was back with me where we belonged.

"Um, Angie?" Charles said, approaching with Nan and Cal at either side. "We can still make the arbitration, if you want to—"

"Let's do it," I said.

Now that I had my best friend at my side, there was no way I would let anyone hurt him ever again. We were back together, and that's how we would stay.

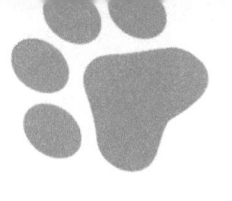

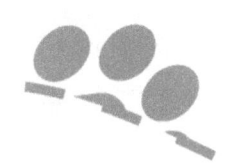

20

"object!" Nan cried when the five of us burst into the county court roughly twenty minutes later.

The nearest clerk waved us over to her window behind a thick layer of plexiglass. "Hello, there. What are we objecting to today?"

Charles pushed himself in front of Nan. "Hi, yes. We're here for the arbitration hearing regarding Ethel Fulton's estate."

The woman nodded her permed head and continued to smile brightly at all of us. "Oh, lots of folks have come in for that one. Room B-2. You're right on time. Good luck."

Before we could stop her, Nan ran down the hall

and flung open the door to Room B-2. "I object!" she cried.

The rest of us ran after her and popped in a second later.

"Longfellow," the person who sat at the front of the room said, fixing Charles with a stern look. "Control your client, and do it now."

We all sat in the back of the room, careful not to make direct eye contact with any of the other heirs. I did a quick scan and saw that Anne was nowhere to be found.

Drats! I still desperately wanted proof that it had been her, and I wanted to make sure she understood the lengths I would go to in order to protect my cat from any future shenanigans on her part.

"Now," the arbiter said, "there have been several challenges to the will of Ethel Fulton, particularly in regards to one Octavius Fulton. Is he here today?"

"Yes, your honor." I rose to my feet with my furry friend in my arms, not sure whether I was addressing the arbiter correctly since this was all a huge first for me.

"Let me guess. Octavius is the cat. Isn't he?" the man asked with a bored expression.

"Yes, but Ethel loved him like a son and wanted

to make sure he was cared for in the manner to which he'd grown accustomed," Charles explained.

"I can see that." The arbiter flipped through the copy of the will in front of him and cracked his neck to either side. He glanced up at us again a few minutes later with a tight-lipped smile. "There are precedents for this. Ethel could have left the entire state of Maine to her cat for all I care. It's not up to the court to question that. So, why are we here?"

"The house," a scratchy voice wheezed from near the door.

Everyone turned, and I about lost my lunch when I saw who was standing there.

Anne Fulton was every bit as frumpy as I remembered. Her gray hair had been cut short, and her arm was freshly bandaged but still bleeding heavily.

"Is that your work?" I whispered to Octo-Cat.

"You bet it is," he answered proudly, then narrowed his gaze on Anne and let out an impressive hiss.

"The house wasn't specifically in the will," the arbiter said.

"Maybe not," Anne said, keeping a great deal of distance between us as she approached the front of the room. "But somehow the cat's still managed to inherit it."

"Actually, the house is mine," I said.

"And mine," Nan added.

"My clients purchased the house from the open market. Their ties to Ethel Fulton's estate are irrelevant," Charles added helpfully. *My hero.*

"I agree," the arbiter said. "Anything else to contest?"

Nobody said anything, but Nan wore a giant, sappy grin. Octo-Cat had hopped into her lap, and she was petting him with slow, leisurely strokes—just the way he liked.

"Then the terms of the will stand as written," the arbiter said. I expected a gavel to bang, but it didn't. Oh, well.

We remained seated until all the Fultons had shuffled out of the room. I was sad to see that my old boss, Richard, hadn't been able to make the trip up from Florida, but happy that this was finally over.

Only Anne remained behind.

"I know it was you," I hissed.

Octo-Cat backed me up with a hiss of his own, too.

"Why did you take my cat?" I demanded, gripping the edges of my chair so I wouldn't be tempted to charge straight up to her and give her the beatdown she deserved.

Anne didn't even look sorry. "That's my aunt Ethel's cat. He should have stayed in the family after she'd gone."

"Him or his trust fund?" Nan shot back. "Because judging by that open wound on your arm, our dear Octavius doesn't want anything to do with the likes of you."

"You can't prove anything," Anne spat. "And you can't do anything, either. So I took a cat for a few days. It's not like I committed murder."

"You're walking on really shaky ground," Nan warned as Octo-Cat jumped off her lap and trotted over to the villainess of the hour.

"I'm going to get that house," Anne mumbled, then grabbed her injured arm and fled through the door right as Oct-Cat was getting ready to take a fresh swipe.

Nan and I exchanged a quick glance, then she tucked her arm into Cal's and said, "C'mon, you handsome thing. I want to thank that kind lady who helped us when we first arrived."

They left through the same door Anne had.

Now only Charles, Octo-Cat, and I remained in the arbitration room.

I sighed and laid my head on Charles's shoulder.

"I'm glad you got him back," he said.

"Me, too."

"Are we going home now?" Octo-Cat whined, waiting for somebody to open the door for him. "I'm absolutely dying for some Evian."

"Soon," I said after making a brusque hushing noise.

Charles shook his head. "Is he seriously complaining again?"

"Yup," I answered with a chuckle, pulling myself back into a full seated position.

Charles turned in his seat to face me more directly. "Well, now that he's back, there's something I've been meaning to say to you for a while now."

I gulped hard as blood rushed through my veins. He had something to say.

Did that mean...?

Was he finally going to...?

Would we...?

He placed a hand on each of my shoulders and

tried to hide his widening smile. "Now I don't want you to take this the wrong way, but..."

"Yes?" I asked, lowering my eyelashes to show him I was ready for his kiss. Heck, I was pretty much ready to marry him on the spot, and we were already at the county court. *I do. I do!*

"Angie," he said softly, then waited for me to re-open my eyes. "You're fired."

My heart dropped all the way down to the floor. He was supposed to kiss me, not fire me!

Charles pressed his forehead to mine, and his warm breaths landed near my nose. "I told you not to take it the wrong way. I'm doing you a favor here. Actually, I'm doing both of us a favor."

"Come again now?" I mumbled, wishing I had something more intelligent to say in that moment.

"I've known you wanted to quit for weeks now. Maybe months. What's stopping you?"

"I didn't want to let you down," I admitted.

He tucked a stray tendril of sandy brown hair behind my ear. "You could never let me down, but I don't want you putting your dreams on hold because of me, either."

He was so impossibly close that it made it hard for me to focus. I still wasn't sure exactly what was happening and whether or not I should be happy about it.

"You're a great P.I., and it's time you went into business for yourself. You can't do that if you're still spending half your days at Longfellow and Associates, so... You're fired."

"Thank you?" I said, guessing at the appropriate response. There may have been precedents regarding Ethel's estate, but what was happening between me and Charles right now was completely and totally new.

He laughed softly. "Don't thank me. I'm doing this for selfish reasons, too."

"Oh?" I asked on a soft exhale. Still so uneasy about how close we were. Still wanting that kiss.

"Yeah, because when I was your boss, I couldn't do this."

I sucked in a deep breath, but before I could let it out, Charles's lips were on mine. Oh my gosh, I was kissing Charles!

And it was everything I'd ever dreamed it would be.

"Humans are disgusting," Octo-Cat complained, taking a swipe at my arm. Thankfully, it was much gentler than the number he'd done on Anne.

Charles laughed as he pulled away. "Let me guess, he didn't like that."

"Yeah," I admitted. "But not because he's jealous, because he thinks it's gross."

Charles rolled his eyes, which just so happened to have happy sparkles in them at the moment. "Whatever, cat. I know you call me UpChuck behind my back."

"Boys, boys," I said, smiling so hard that the corners of my mouth hurt. "You're just going to have to find a way to share."

I stood, and Charles immediately laced his fingers between mine, leaving Octo-Cat to follow behind on foot.

"I can't believe you're choosing to focus on this needless romance when you should be focused on getting me Evian as soon as humanly possible," my cat grumbled predictably.

I scooped him up in my free arm and held him as we walked out of the courthouse. "When we get home, there's someone very special I want you to meet."

"Ugh, why? I'm so tired," he whined.

"He's the president of your fan club," I revealed, picturing how insanely happy Pringle would be to meet his idol.

"Can I be the president of your fan club?" Charles asked, giving my hand a squeeze.

I pretended to think about this for a moment. "I don't really need a fan club, but you can be my boyfriend. That is if you—"

Charles stopped walking, pulled me close, and kissed me again.

I took that to mean he agreed.

A tiny rescue dog. A spoiled house cat. A big mystery to solve.

Get your copy of *Chihuahua Conspiracy,* so that you can keep reading this series today!

Pssst... If you absolutely loved this book and want even more, make sure you **sign up for Molly's newsletter**. When you do, you'll receive an exclusive digital prize pack, including a free book!

WHAT'S NEXT?

My crazy old Nan loves making decisions on a whim. Last week, she took up flamenco dancing. This week, she's adopted a trouble-making Chihuahua named Paisley. This wouldn't be much of a problem, were it not for the very crabby tabby who also lives with us.

Man, I never thought I'd miss hearing Octo-Cat's voice, but his silent protest is becoming too much to bear, especially since we just opened our new P.I. business together.

Things go from bad to worse, of course, when Nan and I discover that someone has been embezzling funds from the local animal shelter. If we can't find the culprit soon, the shelter may not be able to keep its lights on and those poor homeless pets won't have anywhere to go.

Okay, so I just need to find the thief, rescue the animals, and save the day—all while trying to find a way for Octo-Cat and Paisley to set aside their differences and work together as a team. Yeah, wish me luck...

CHIHUAHUA CONSPIRACY is now available.

Get your copy so that you can keep reading this series today!

SNEAK PEEK

CHIHUAHUA CONSPIRACY

Hi, I'm Angie Russo, and this last year has been quite the wild ride for me. Yes, it's been exactly one year since my entire life changed for the better.

Sure, I've come face-to-face with a lot of dangerous characters lately—murderers, kidnappers, creeps, you name it—but I wouldn't trade my life for anyone else's.

Here's the deal... It all started at my former job as a paralegal.

A wealthy old woman had just died, and her heirs had gathered at our office for the official Will reading. I was instructed to make coffee, and, well, that was the last time I ever attempted such a dangerous feat.

You see, I got electrocuted and knocked unconscious. I woke up with a wicked fear of coffee makers and, oh, also the ability to talk to animals. At first, I could only talk to this one cat named Octavius Maxwell Ricardo Edmund Frederick Fulton. He was one of the primary beneficiaries of his late owner's estate, and I now call him Octo-Cat for short.

Long story short, he told me the old lady was murdered and begged me to help him catch the killer. We did, and we pretty much became best friends in the process. Now he lives with me, and I oversee his care and also his generous trust fund.

And because I accidentally made an open-ended deal with him when I needed to get him to wear a pet harness, we now reside in his former owner's exquisite manor house. Yes, a ten-dollar neon green harness ended up costing me a cool million.

At least most of the money was my cat's, anyway.

Yeah. A lot has happened over the last year. My cat and I solved three more murders together. He got catnapped. I finally quit my paralegal job so we could open up a private investigation firm together, and oh, yeah... I got a boyfriend!

My nan might be even more excited about that one than I am. She'd been trying to matchmake me for years, and now that she's finally succeeded, she's not quite sure what to do with herself.

Yes, she continues to bake up a storm in the kitchen and take her community art classes, but lately she's also been flipping through new hobbies like they're going out of style. There's been flamenco dancing, learning Korean as a second language, even Pokémon Go. She claims Pikachu understands her on a spiritual level. Personally, I don't get it.

My mom and dad are busy with their jobs as Blueberry Bay's local news anchor and designated sports guy. Nan and I have them over once per week for a nice home-cooked meal. Did I mention my grandmother and I live together?

It's not weird. She's not just the woman who raised me, but she's also my best friend and the most amazing person I know. She even helps with Octo-Cat's lavish demands and rigorous schedule.

And between the two of us, we keep him dining on only the seafood flavors of Fancy Feast and drinking Evian from his favorite Lenox teacup.

Most recently, he's demanded a brand new iPad

Pro. His reasoning? That he needed a professional upgrade to go along with our new business venture. Never mind that he uses his tablet primarily to play various fish tank and koi pond games.

He's given his old device to the president of his fan club, a raccoon who lives under our front porch. His name is Pringle, and he's a pretty all right guy most of the time. Octo-Cat definitely enjoys having a fanboy to support every single decision he makes, including his regular criticism of me.

It's true. Octo-Cat complains a lot, but I also know he loves me tons. That's why I'm planning a special evening to celebrate our petaversary. I'm not sure he remembers, but after tonight he will.

I can't wait to see the look on his little kitty face when he sees what I have planned for him. Let the games begin!

It wasn't easy hiding my party preparation from Octo-Cat, but so far he hadn't managed to catch on. Rather than cooking something myself, I asked Nan to pick up some grilled shrimp and lobster rolls from the Little Dog Diner in Misty Cove. It's a bit of a drive, but worth every mile.

Nan would be returning any minute, which meant it was time for me to wake the guest of honor. I found him sleeping in his five o'clock sunspot on the western side of the house. "Wakey, wakey!" I cried in a sing-song voice he loathed.

"Angela," he groaned, "haven't you ever heard that you should let sleeping cats lie?"

"I'm pretty sure the expression is—you know what? It doesn't matter. C'mon, I have a surprise for you."

Whoa, close one. I almost used the word dog in a sentence. That little slipup would have ruined our whole night, but I caught myself just in time.

"A surprise?" he asked, yawning so wide that his whiskers overlapped in front of his nose. "What is it?"

"You'll see. C'mon." I patted my leg and motioned for him to follow.

But he sat his butt back down on the hardwood floor and flicked his tail. "Tell me, or I'm not coming," he demanded.

"Octo-Cat, can't you just—Ugh, fine. Today marks one year since we first met. Do you remember that day?"

"So you mean it's been one year and one day

since Ethel died?" he asked, raising his eyebrows and staring me down.

Oh, I didn't think of that. I hoped he wouldn't be too sad to celebrate.

"I'm just giving you a hard time," he said with a cruel laugh, trotting over as he shook his head. "Happy anniversary, Angela. I'm glad you're my human."

Footsteps sounded on the porch. I hadn't even heard Nan pull up, but now she was here, and we could officially begin our little party. I'd asked my boyfriend, Charles, to wait a couple hours before he turned up, since he and Octo-Cat didn't get along particularly well as of late.

I secretly loved that my cat was jealous of my boyfriend but hoped that he'd eventually get over it.

"Nan?" I called when Octo-Cat and I reached the bottom of the stairs, but she still hadn't entered. Padding over to the door, I twisted the knob and—

A wagging ball of black fur pounced into the house.

"I'm here! I'm home! Oh, boy. Oh, boy. Oh, boy!" the little dog cried, then immediately squatted and peed on the welcome mat.

I turned to Octo-Cat who stood on the last stair with his back arched and his tail at full-blown puffball status. "Angela, what is this?" he screamed, unwittingly drawing the dog's attention over to him.

"A cat! A cat! Oh, boy! Oh, boy! Oh, boy!" The dog, who upon closer examination appeared to be a Chihuahua, bounded right up to Octo-Cat and pressed his nose to the cat's butt.

Octo-Cat hissed, growled, swiped with his claws, and sent the little dog shrieking away.

Yipe! Yipe! Yipe!

"What's all this commotion?" Nan asked, charging into the house, spotting the little black dog and scooping the poor, whimpering baby into her arms. "Okay, fess up. Who hurt my Paisley?"

"Nan..." I pinched the bridge of my nose to stave off the rapidly building headache. "Why is there a dog in our house?"

"This is Paisley. Yes, she is," Nan cooed in a baby voice, and the Chihuahua licked her cheek, the horrible scary cat and the pain he'd inflicted apparently forgotten. "She lives here now."

"Oh, heck no!" Octo-Cat shouted from his spot on the stairs. "I thought we were celebrating me tonight, not taking a visit to the ninth circle of hell!"

"Nan," I said trying to make peace before

everyone lost their cool. "We can't have a dog here. Octo-Cat hates dogs."

"Hatesssssss," Octo-Cat hissed, then growled again.

"He hates me?" the shivering, little dog asked. "He doesn't even know me. I'm Paisley, and I'm a good girl."

Nan continued to talk in a goochie-goo voice, keeping her eyes glued to the mostly black tri-color Chihuahua in her arms. "Well, I saw this little girl at the shelter and right away she stole my heart. What was I supposed to do?"

She looked up and narrowed her eyes on me. "Was I supposed to let her stay in that cage all by herself? Or, Heaven forbid, let them put her down when the shelter got too full?" She covered Paisley's oversized ears and frowned at me.

"No, I mean..." I sputtered. "No, of course you couldn't do that." Ack, I was such a softie.

"Octavius is just going to have to get used to his new housemate, because I'm not taking her back," Nan said in a way that made it more than clear that this topic was not up for discussion. "C'mon, baby, let's go outside and meet the forest creatures."

Once Nan and Paisley were safely outside, I

searched around for Octo-Cat so I could both explain and apologize on Nan's behalf.

But he was nowhere to be found.

Crud, he was never going to forgive me for this one.

CHIHUAHUA CONSPIRACY is now available.

Get your copy so that you can keep reading this series today!

ABOUT MOLLY FITZ

While *USA Today bestselling* author Molly Fitz can't technically talk to animals, she and her three feline writing assistants have deep and very animated conversations as they navigate their days.

She lives with her child and their own private zoo somewhere in the wilds of Alaska. Molly will occasionally venture out for good food, great coffee, or to meet new animal friends.

Learn more about Molly and her books, and be sure to sign up for her newsletter at **www.Molly Mysteries.com**.

ALSO BY MOLLY FITZ

Learn more about Molly's collected works, so that you can decide which book you'd like to read next...

PET WHISPERER P.I.

Angie Russo just partnered up with Blueberry Bay's first ever talking cat detective. Along with his ragtag gang of human and animal helpers, Octo-Cat is determined to save the day... so long as it doesn't interfere with his schedule.

Start with book 1, ***Kitty Confidential***.

MERLIN'S MAGICAL MYSTERIES

Gracie Springs is not a witch... but her cat is. Now she must help to keep his secret or risk spending the rest of her life in some magical prison. Too bad trouble seems to find them at every turn!

Start with book 1, ***Merlin Takes a Familiar***.

PARANORMAL TEMP AGENCY

Tawny Bigford's simple life takes a turn for the magical when she stumbles upon her landlady's murder and is recruited by a talking black cat named Fluffikins to take over the deceased's role as the official Town Witch for Beech Grove, Georgia.

Start with book 1, ***Witch for Hire***.

THE MYSTERIES OF MOONLIGHT MANOR (WITH TRIXIE SILVERTALE)

Sydney Coleman has it all—until she doesn't. No sooner does she launch her bed and breakfast, than a trio of ghosts turn up oppose her at every turn. They insist she solve the murder of their mistress, but Sydney is desperate for cash. If she can't book some guests fast, her haunted mansion is utterly doomed.

Start with book 1, ***Moonlight & Mischief***.

CONNECT WITH MOLLY

Sign up for my newsletter and get a special digital prize pack for joining, including an exclusive story, *Meowy Christmas Mayhem*, fun quiz, and lots of cat pictures!

Sign up: **MollyMysteries.com/subscribe**

Now, if you ever wished you could converse with cats, here's your opportunity! This is me officially inviting you into my whacky inner world as part of my Cozy Kitty Book Club.

For those who just can't get enough of my zany cat characters and their hapless humans, this book club will provide new content to devour and the chance to get to know my best author friends.

From exclusive stories, behind-the-scenes trivia to never-before-released bonus content, and monthly giveaways, there's a lot to love about the Cozy Kitty Book Club. Join today to find out what we're reading next!

Join: **MollyMysteries.com/club**